BENEDICTION DENIED

ALSO BY ELIZABETH ENGSTROM

When Darkness Loves Us
Black Ambrosia
Nightmare Flower
Lizzie Borden
Lizard Wine
The Alchemy of Love
Suspicions
Black Leather
Candyland
The Northwoods Chronicles
York's Moon
Something Happened to Grandma
Baggage Check
How to Write a Sizzling Sex Scene

Word by Word (editor, with John Tullius)
Imagination Fully Dilated (co-editor)
Imagination Fully Dilated vol. II (editor)
Dead on Demand (editor)
Pronto! Writings from Rome (editor, with John Tullius)
Ship's Log: Writings at Sea (editor, with John Tullius)
Lies and Limericks (editor, with John Tullius)
Mota 9: Addiction (editor)

Benediction Denied

A Labyrinth of Souls Novel

by

Elizabeth Engstrom

ShadowSpinners Press

This book is dedicated, of course, to my sweet husband, Al Cratty. Thank you for marrying me and making my home life a warm and serene place to be.

ACKNOWLEDGEMENTS

It's hard to imagine that one person could actually write an entire book without a long lifetime of influences. My personality and proclivities have been formed by family, friends, teachers, mentors, and experiences—horrific, sublime, and most everything between. My great thanks to all of the above and more, most particularly the very patient Al Cratty, Wordcrafters in Eugene, the Ghost Story Weekend gang, and Matthew Lowes for the genius of the Labyrinth of Souls.

EDITOR'S PREFACE

Dungeon Solitaire: Labyrinth of Souls is a fantasy game for tarot cards, written by Matthew Lowes and Illustrated by Josephe Vandel. In the game you defeat monsters, disarm traps, open doors, and explore mazes as you delve the depths of a dangerous dungeon. Along the way you collect treasure and magic items, gain skills, and gather companions.

Now ShadowSpinners Press is publishing this and other stand-alone novels inspired by the game. Each *Labyrinth of Souls* novel features a journey into a unique vision of the underworld.

The Labyrinth of Souls is more than an ancient ruin filled with monsters, trapped treasure, and the lost tombs of bygone kings. It is a manifestation of a mythic underworld, existing at a crossroads between people and cultures, between time and space, between the physical world and the deepest reaches of the psyche. It is a dark mirror held up to human experience, in which you may find your dreams … or your doom. Entrances to this realm can appear in any time period, in any location. There are innumerable reasons why a person may enter, but it is a place antagonistic to those who do, a place where monsters dwell, with obstacles and illusions to waylay adventurers, and whose very walls can be a force of corruption. It is a haunted place, ever at the edge of sanity.

BENEDICTION DENIED

1

ADAM SWAN STRUGGLED UP through dark, painful layers of consciousness. Way in the back of his awareness, he knew that full consciousness would mean full pain. He resisted, wishing desperately to sink into blissful sleep, but he didn't think his sleep had been all that blissful, and he couldn't find anything to cling to in order to help him get there.

His head pounded so hard it actually moved with each heartbeat. He not only saw the red pulses behind his closed eyes, but he heard each heart beat thundering through what surely must be a broken skull.

He brought his knees to his chest and cradled his arms over his exploding head.

He was lying on his side. He tried to imagine where he was, how he got there, but he had no room for anything but the pounding, the thundering hammering in his head. There was a very real possibility that the top of his head could blow off with the pressure of each raging beat of his pulse.

He grabbed his head with both hands and squeezed. The dirt beneath him moved, too.

Dirt floor.

What the hell?

He cracked an eye open, bringing with it harsh, jagged waves of pain. Although there was very little light, he saw walls.

At least he was alive.

Gritting his teeth against the pain, he moved around to assess the damage. His arms worked. His hands worked. They didn't seem to be injured. He flexed his shoulders.

It was just his head.

He reached around with a tentative touch and picked off crusty dried blood above his ear. Probing fingers found a lump the size of a lemon.

Slowly, carefully testing, he moved his feet, then his legs. One knee gave him some grief, but nothing like his head.

He squinted his eyes, then opened them just a tiny bit, adjusted his glasses, and looked around.

A dark room. Dirt floor. Indistinct light coming from above. He pushed on his temples, trying to arrest the pain, scooted to a wall and pushed himself up to a sitting position, leaning against the wall. Wooden wall.

He stopped moving and closed his eyes again, seeing red and yellow starbursts of pain emanate from his cracked skull until they seemed to fill the room. The pounding lessened when he was still, quiet, not moving.

After a long moment, he carefully opened his eyes again and looked around, gently moving his head, assessing any damage that might have been done to his neck, trying desperately not to start the shattering waves of pain that threatened to shoot his eyeballs right out of their sockets.

Dirt floor. Small, square room. Door at one end. Vent in the roof, the source of the light. Hot. Steamy. Jungle. Still in the jungle. Still in Congo. Stench of urine. Bucket in the corner, perhaps the source of the stench.

Small table next to the wall.

He closed his eyes and tried to relax. Tried to remember.

Oh!

The memory of saying goodbye to his wife at the airport startled him. He twitched and sent fresh shockwaves through his fragile cranium.

He'd put his family on the plane home. He, a hydraulic engineer with the Justice Corps, would stay another three months to finish the water system he and his local helpers were installing. He'd been here for six months, working in the jungle and he wouldn't leave until he was certain the system would work the way they had engineered it.

His family—wife and three daughters—had come to visit for the summer.

And then …

And then, as he returned to the village from the airport, along the rutted dirt road, two beat up and muddy pickup trucks blocked the way. He stopped the Jeep and reached for his passport and NGO identification card from the glove compartment.

Two big men with guns stepped out of the jungle, opened the Jeep door, grabbed him by the shirt and pulled him out, papers in hand.

One of them grabbed his ID.

"Water man?" he asked.

Adam knew about the rebels, of course, criminals that ran guns, made snuff films, trafficked in women, and sold anything illegal they could get their hands on. They seemed to be some kind of paramilitary force, but nobody really knew their mission, except to terrorize the locals. Adam and his crew had had no interaction with them at all. The only way he knew about them was at his initial orientation session, but their impact on his mission had been minimized. Jolmy and some of the village elders occasionally talked of the thugs, but the bad guys seemed to stay away from the village. There was nothing of value for them there.

And now, here they were. Adam struggled not to panic, but to remember what he was told about how to deal with them.

Be polite. Be firm. Answer questions. Don't antagonize them. Don't challenge them. Just do what they want and they will leave you alone.

Adam put the most innocent look he knew how to manage on his face. "Pardon me? Excuse me?"

The big one with the military shirt, big gun and evil eyes grabbed him by the shirt front and pulled him close. Adam smelled his rotten breath and the jungle body odor on his filthy, sweat-stained uniform. "You water man, yes?"

Adam nodded. "Yes, yes. Water man."

"Very valuable," the rebel said to the others.

Adam realized where this was going. He held up his hands in protest. "No, no, not valuable. Volunteer. No pay."

"American." The kidnapper shoved him backwards, someone else tripped him, and Adam hit the dirt.

Another thug climbed into the Jeep.

"Hey, no, hey, that's my Jeep. It belongs—"

Adam saw someone else come at him from the side. He looked up just in time to see a black baton come down at his head.

And now this.

So they would try to ransom him. The Justice Corps wouldn't pay. They had no money. The American government wouldn't pay. They didn't negotiate with terrorists. Chrissie's family had money, but not the kind of money these animals would be demanding.

He'd seen it all in the movies. Soon, if the money to support their rebel government coup—or whatever their organization was about—didn't come because he wasn't as valuable as they wanted him to be, he would be more trouble than he was worth. If they didn't kill him outright, they'd likely just leave him here in this makeshift jail cell to starve.

Or die of a broken skull.

He gritted his teeth and let his fingers gently explore the enormous lump behind his ear. It seemed to be just a knot. He gingerly touched the split in the skin again. Blood had leaked down the back of his neck, but it hadn't been severe. If his skull hadn't been fractured, if he had just been knocked out by that baton, then the pain should eventually subside.

He pulled his feet up, then tipped over onto his side, his back to the wall. He would sleep, if he could, and when he awoke, the pain wouldn't be so bad. He was strong and healthy. He would heal.

He closed his eyes and thought of his wife and girls. They had enjoyed their summer in Congo. They should be getting back to Minneapolis soon, excited and ready for the new school year.

The summer had gone by quickly.

Adam was busy working on the water system, and didn't spend as much time with them as he wanted to. The system wasn't complicated, but the little village, way out in the bush, miles from anywhere, had grown up next to a river. With climate change and political fighting upriver over water rights, the river had, over time, changed course. Now, the villagers had to walk over an hour for their daily water.

Adam's company loaned him to the Justice Corps to join a team that designed a simple system to bring water to the remote village. The system may have been simple, but it had its issues.

After numerous tries, they finally dug a well that hit a good aquifer between the village and the river. The water tested potable, but laying that much pipe proved problematic. Those details were left to Jolmy, Adam's foreman, who employed the local men to dig the trenches. Adam worked on the pump assembly, the holding tanks, the filtration devices, all the other things that went into a solar-powered water system out in the bush.

While Adam worked, Chrissie and the girls found much to entertain and intrigue them, making friends, learning new things. Adam knew it would be an excellent cultural experience for them all, and he had been right.

The small village was home to about a hundred fifty people, most of them children, it seemed. This year there were seven Justice Corps volunteers: four on Adam's crew, and three teachers.

In some way each of his girls had been a help to the village elders and the other Justice Corps volunteers.

Chrissie, Adam's wife, spent her days sewing shirts, skirts, and dresses on an old treadle sewing machine left behind by some other NGO group. As she worked, she taught the local women how to use the machine, how to use their clothes to make patterns for new clothes, and then to stitch them up. She brought a small stash of beading materials and taught beading skills to a little knot of interested local women, and took home a whole box full of handcrafted jewelry to sell for them. These women were all excited with the prospect of a small export business that could benefit their families and the village economy.

Adam loved seeing her talking and laughing with her circle of friends while babies crawled around the floor in the kitchen tent, and the older children played just outside. He was delighted that each family member fell into the culture with such ease. Well, almost each family member.

Lisa, fifteen, had been a help to one of the teachers, helping to teach English, reading, and writing to the older children. Lisa was the writer and poet in the group, the science nerd of the family, but as an introvert, she didn't bond with her peers as well. She was happy to teach the younger children while she counted down the days to going home.

By contrast, Sonja, twelve, had made very close friends. She was always busy in the kitchen, helping Belvina, Jolmy's wife, prepare meals, learning how to cook on a wood-fired stove, how to bake in a wood-fired oven.

If she wasn't in the kitchen or helping Belvina in the little kitchen garden, Sonja was out fooling around with her friends, playing games and sharing the secrets that twelve year old girls all have to share with one another. They all hugged and cried when she got into the Jeep with her little flowered backpack, headed for home.

Mouse, the youngest at ten, loved the jungle. She was quite the wild thing, completely different from her older sisters. She was dark haired, adventurous, and always getting herself into trouble. Officially named Monica Sue Swan, Adam's father had immediately re-christened her Mouse before they were even out of the birthing center, and that name stuck. She had been quite a challenge in the village, not at all interested in abiding by the local customs and standards of behavior. After a while, Adam and Chrissie soon realized that Mouse had many aunties to keep an eye on her. She was not the first daring child the village elders had seen. Eventually, she survived all her forays into places she shouldn't be, playing with creatures she should be leaving alone, and tasting things that weren't edible.

Overall, Adam and Chrissie were very proud of their girls—the Swan Sisters. He missed them the minute he hugged them all goodbye at the little airport.

A pang of homesickness set off a new set of painful waves in his vision.

Were they home by now?

No, they wouldn't be home yet, not for a couple of days.

But how long had he been here? Did anybody know yet that he was missing? Had his captors made their ransom demands to the Justice Corps?

If he didn't return, the superstitious locals would begin to spread rumors that he had been kidnapped by jealous gods and taken into the underworld.

In addition to designing and helping to build their potable water system, Adam's supervisor asked him to teach Sunday School, since there wasn't currently a missionary or a chaplain on site. Preaching was not his strong suit, but he tried. The best he could do was help the villagers see Christianity as an adjunct to their superstitions about the strange forces that dwelt beneath their feet. The locals, most of whom knew more about Christianity than he did, found it faintly amusing, the prospect of an invisible, good, Christian god above and an invisible, bad, superstitious god below, yet neither one helped get fresh water to drink or medicine for their sick children. He had to agree. What would be the purpose of an all-powerful god if people got sick and died?

Adam considered himself a man of faith, so he tried to teach them, avoiding the difficult theological questions, and he tried to learn from them, particularly Jolmy, his foreman on the water crew, who was happy to counter

Adam's Christian stories with strange stories of his own faith.

The village library, in addition to the raggedy collection of worn and torn children's books, had an old, shabby Lutheran hymnal, so he used that to teach them songs, and create his sermons, which he kept very simple.

Sonja encouraged the other children to put on little dances and skits that went along with some basic Bible stories, to the delight of everyone. Such festivities were always followed by a communal feast.

Sunday became a time of joy, a respite from the work week, and Adam was happy to be a part of it.

"Please, God," Adam whispered out loud in his cell of unimaginable pain. "I've tried to be a good man. Have mercy on me."

❧

Adam startled awake at the sound of a car door slamming. Outside his prison cell, men argued about something in loud, angry voices.

He sat up, adrenaline pumping through his system. Though his head still pounded, it no longer threatened to crack open at the slightest motion, and he took a moment to be grateful for that.

If the men were angry, was it because they found out they would get no money for him? Would they come in and kill him outright?

He looked around for something he could use as a weapon.

He had nothing in his pockets. His wallet, cell phone, and pen knife had all been taken away.

A low table sat across the room in the corner. Perhaps he could break it up and use it as a weapon.

Carefully, he stood on unsteady, trembling legs and made his way across the room.

Rumbles of pain surged through his head, but fear cleared his eyesight.

The table was more like a little step stool, the short legs maybe eight inches long. Not much of a weapon. On top of the table was a deck of cards.

Very odd.

He picked up the cards with one hand, and picked up the table with the other. It was very light. He could throw the whole table at someone, but what good would that do? That petty act of aggression would surely only infuriate the thugs who had kidnapped him.

He set the table down in the middle of the room, then sat on it, facing the door, ready. His senses rose to full alert. He was ready for whatever was about to come through that door, whatever that meant.

Could he rush the thug and escape?

No, of course not. There were several others out there, arguing.

He was definitely feeling better, but would sell his soul for a drink of fresh water. Perhaps if he was compliant, they would treat him well.

He waited, mindlessly shuffling the deck of cards in his hands. They weren't any kind of cards he knew about. These had pictures on them.

Chain links jangled on the other side of the door. A lock opened.

His heart pounded in anticipation.

His head pounded in time with his heart.

The door swung open.

The silhouette of a large man stood against the twilight.

"Up!" the man approached him, brandishing what looked like the same baton that had cracked his head earlier.

Adam stood on shaky legs.

The huge man approached with purposeful strides.

Adam stepped back, overturning the table. With another step back, he tripped on the table and went down hard, landing on his back.

The man raised the baton, baring his teeth in a horrifying grimace that exuded meanness. He took another step forward.

Adam scrambled away from the menacing figure, but he had no defense.

He pulled a card from the top of the deck in his hand. Wishing it was metal with a razor edge, he flicked it at the man.

It wasn't a razor, but when it hit the man in the chest, bright blue concentric rings of light banged through the small room. The concussion popped Adam's ears.

The man looked startled by Adam's aggression, but Adam had only a moment to notice.

He was falling.

His stomach lurched. He struggled not to puke. He flailed, but he was still on his back on the ground. Secure.

The man in front of him was getting bigger, and bigger yet.

No. Adam was getting smaller.

Nausea overwhelmed him, but he choked down the bile that rose in his throat as the elevator plunge stopped. He looked up, not only at the giant of a man in front of him, but the man's enormous boot and the overturned table that was now taller than he was.

That boot could crush him.

In spite of the pain in his head, Adam sprang to his feet and ran toward the closest wall, the corner where the table had originally sat. He found a hole in the dirt floor, under the wall, clearly a hole some rodent had dug, big enough for him to run into.

He glanced back at the massive rebel, who was bending down with his giant meaty hand, reaching to grab him.

Adam ducked and ran into the hole. He tripped, rolled, got to his feet, and continued running down what seemed to be a tunnel. His head screamed with pain as the floor of the tunnel shook with every kick the thug gave to the entrance, roaring in frustration.

Adam ran blindly in the dark, desperate to be away from his captors and certain death by that man, with that baton, and that giant boot, in that cell.

2

ADAM RAN UNTIL he could run no more. His lungs ached, his head ready to explode. He stopped, bent over, hands on his knees, and gasped for breath.

After a few moments, the pounding pain in his head began to abate, his heart rate returned to normal, and he could breathe.

He listened.

Silence.

Nobody had followed him. He had run far enough to get away—they'd have to dig to get to him, and likely he wasn't worth it.

Besides … he was … small?

Could that be right?

What kind of a hallucination was this?

He put the deck of cards in the cargo pocket of his pants, then ran his hands over the wall of the tunnel. Dirt. He scratched at it with his fingernails. Dirt. He reached for the top of the tunnel. His fingertips barely grazed it. It, too, was dirt.

He walked slowly along the tunnel in absolute darkness, hands trailing along the wall. It had been dug long ago. Layered fungus grew in patches. Roots and sticks protruded from the walls and hung down from the ceiling. Some roots were a handful thick.

It was hot and steamy.

What the hell?

Was he in the fabled underworld of the village superstitions?

Jolmy frequently spoke of the dark magic and its connection to the underworld. Adam listened with half an ear as Jolmy talked about the underworld gods.

"There is one big one. One big guy," Jolmy said. "He is the king of the underworld."

Adam kept working, cementing PVC pipe joints together.

He didn't approve of that talk, didn't believe in magic or underworld dark gods, and didn't particularly want Jolmy and his family to be telling these tales to his girls.

"He like white meat," Jolmy said, and then laughed. "He would eat you for a snack." He cut another length of pipe, checked the plans laid out on a sheet of plywood on sawhorses, and measured it again, just to be sure.

"Superstition," Adam countered.

"He has helpers. A queen and servants. Plenty servants to do his dirty work. They torment. Torment is what they do." Jolmy stopped sawing and turned to look at Adam. "They rule the sun and the moon."

"Now you know that's not true."

"Not this sun and moon. The underground has its own sun and moon. And stars. And justice! Yes, oh yes, they have their own systems of justice. They would have such fun with you."

Adam gave his best disapproving look.

Jolmy put his head back and laughed so hard he had to wipe his eyes. Then he went back to sawing pipe. "Yes, oh yes," he said. "They would have such fun with you. You best stay above the ground."

"I intend to."

Jolmy laughed again.

In retrospect, that laugh seemed to be a knowing laugh, as if there was no way Adam was going to be able to stay above ground if the king of the underworld wanted him for a snack.

And here he was, underground.

Not only that, but he was the size of a rat, able to run along a tunnel certainly dug by some type of African rodent.

He tried to remember what Jolmy had told him about the underworld and its dark magic.

He had been strong on emotion, but short on details. *He make you cry like a little baby. He make you beg to give up your mother in your place. He decide whether you live or die. He decide what torments you must have. Oh yes, you better stay out of his kingdom.* While Jolmy liked working with Adam, enjoyed Adam's company, he also seemed delighted to imagine a thin, lily-white hydrologist at the mercy of his big, powerful, underworld forces.

But when pressed for details, Jolmy didn't have any personal experience. He didn't know anyone who had encountered these demons, but there were stories. He had heard and oft repeated stories of men who fell into holes, cracks in the earth, crevasses, or went into caves exploring, and came back with terrible stories of how they were teased and tormented and barely escaped with their lives.

And of course there were the stories of men who merely disappeared, never to be seen again.

Dark magic.

Adam chalked it all up to superstitious nonsense, and the fact that Congo had been ruled by dark "kings" for centuries. Surely there were myriad stories made up by the powerless about the powerful.

And yet. Dark Magic.

How else could Adam have shrunk to such a small size? Is that what has just happened?

He sat down, leaned back against the wall of the tunnel. His jungle-appropriate light cotton clothes stuck to him with perspiration.

Surely this was a dream. It had all the dreamlike qualities—but isn't that what the men he worked with said about their underworld? If you get caught in the kingdom of the underworld, if you are lucky, you can dream yourself back to safety. If you cannot do that, you will be lost forever.

Adam dug his heels into the soil. It had been packed down hard, likely from the feet of hundreds, or thousands of creatures using it as a highway.

He saw no creatures. He smelled nothing but the dank earth, yet he saw flickers of movement out of the corners of his eyes. Those had to be dream hallucinations because the darkness was absolute.

To prove it, he brought one hand up in front of his face. Nothing. He could see absolutely nothing.

And he could hear nothing but the blood pounding in his head.

But there it was again. A blue flicker of movement to the left, almost like the spark of static electricity.

Adam used his shirttail to wipe the perspiration from his face. He checked the wound on his head to make certain it had not opened, and then got back to his feet.

If this was a dream, he would have to find a safe place to dream himself home.

If this wasn't a dream, he would have to be very careful, because something had dug this tunnel, and plenty of somethings used it on a regular basis.

There it was again, to the right, that slight indication of movement.

If he walked to the right, toward that movement, he would walk right back into his prison.

He began to walk to the left, trying not to look behind him, just walking as quickly as he could, carefully picking up his feet so as to not stumble on the irregular ground.

The soil of the tunnel had a sound-muffling quality, yet after a moment he recognized a presence behind him, and within a few moments, he could hear it. Worse, he could smell it.

Skunky.

It was catching up to him on soft feet, padding along quickly toward him.

He heard it breathe.

His head began to ache again.

He began to run, holding his hands out in front of him, but the thing behind him, perhaps sensing that prey was ahead, began to close in.

Adam's feet pounded the ground, his breath rasped in his dry throat and he heard himself making little sounds in spite of trying to be as invisible as possible. It didn't matter. He smelled like human blood and sweat. If he was being pursued by a predator, he was done for.

Were there even skunks in Africa? There were weasels, he knew. At his size, they would be the size of lions. Nothing to mess with.

It was catching up to him, and he could run no faster.

He stopped and turned, armed with … nothing.

No, not nothing.

He stood his ground and reached into his pocket. He couldn't see the card in the dark, but when the creature came upon him, felt its hot breath, smelled its skunk stench, the brush of gigantic whiskers across his face, he flung the card at it as hard as he could.

Blue concentric shockwaves illuminated a giant black and white mongoose, with surprise on its triangular face. The creature squeaked and backed off, its eyes shiny, its nose twitching. Its teeth seemed to be as big as the fence posts Adam had installed up in the village. It would have no trouble eating him. The villagers battled mongoose daily for the lives of the chickens.

He turned again to run, and in the fading light of the shockwave, he saw what looked like a hard edge up ahead.

With the sniffing creature again closing in on him, he got to the edge, gripped it and desperately tried to identify it, tried to find a way to use it to either hide from or repel the mongoose.

Metal. Metal bars. A gate!

Whiskers raked across his back as he finally found a latch, clicked it, and the gate opened. He slipped through and slammed it behind him.

The mongoose stopped and sniffed, pawed at the metal gate, like a cage door. It dug a little bit at the soft ground underneath the door, sniffed, snorted, pawed some more.

Adam reached through the bars and punched the weasel on the nose.

It squeaked, backed off, then dug a little more, before giving up and continuing on its way down the tunnel.

Adam fell to his knees, weak with fear and pain and exhaustion.

He prayed to God to either wake him from his horrible nightmare, or to provide a way out.

After a few moments, he realized that before he could rest, before he could let his guard down, lest another mongoose—or worse—came by, he needed to investigate the room, or the cell, or whatever it was that he was in.

It seemed to be just another tunnel.

Regardless, he seemed to be alone, and the gate was closed securely behind him.

Wait a minute. A gate? What the hell was a metal gate doing in a rat tunnel?

He didn't care. He was safe for the moment.

He sat down, mopped his face, caught his breath, then pulled the deck of cards from his pocket and began to shuffle them.

These things were the stuff of dreams. Magic. Magic cards. He threw one at danger and the shockwaves of magic got him out of trouble. At least it got him out of imminent danger. He was still in trouble.

He had thirty-one cards left.

But how did they work? Did different cards provide different results? Was this dark magic?

He knew from reading books to his girls, particularly to Mouse, who was in love with fantasy novels, that there was always a price to pay for using magic.

So not only did he not understand the rules of this magic as it was to be used, but he didn't know the cost he was going to pay every time he threw a card at a problem.

Was it evil? Was he using evil?

He put the cards back into his pants pocket, keeping them safe, keeping them close.

And then he prayed. He got on his knees, hoping that God would see that as a sincere gesture. He folded his hands as he taught his daughters to do. He closed his eyes and whispered, "Please, God. I've not been the best human being you ever created. I'm not the best husband, the best father, or even the best hydrologist, but I try."

Even as he whispered this out loud, he hoped that God was hearing his words and not looking into his heart.

"I ask you, God of mercies, please help me get out of this very strange situation that cannot be of you, cannot be your will. To be the size of a rat and relegated to a dark tunnel is surely not your will for my life. If you see me through this—or see that I wake up from this horrible nightmare, I promise to serve you as never before. I promise to be the best husband, and father, and altruistic human being. Please, Father, I beg of you."

His words sounded hollow and trite.

Oh.

"In Jesus' name I pray."

That should seal the deal.

He sat back and took a deep breath. With God's help, he would get out of here, get back to the village to tell a *real* tale to Jolmy about the *real* underworld. And how his *real* God, his *Christian* God, had saved him.

Then he would go home to his family and hug his girls.

He would be a better husband and father. He had faltered on both those counts, as was evidenced by the truth of what happened when he dropped his girls at the airport. Mouse grabbed her backpack and immediately ran into the little one-room terminal without even saying goodbye to him. Sonja chased her to keep her out of trouble. Lisa gave him a perfunctory kiss on the cheek, and Chrissie took her bag from him, no kiss, not even a goodbye. She just turned and followed the girls into the terminal.

He deserved the cold shoulder from all of them.

But then who was perfect? Who was a perfect father? He'd seen Jolmy get overly angry with his wife and one or another of his children.

There were no perfect parents.

In time, his wife and children would remember fondly the time they spent their summer in Congo.

A moan escaped his lips as he remembered how they sought his attention during their three months in the village, but he was too busy with either work or playing cards with his village friends who let the women do the women's work. He had been way too eager to buy into that.

He was a wretch, but he didn't have to be. And he would get out of here and make amends to his girls.

"Amazing grace ..." he whispered.

Adam tipped over onto his side, drew his knees up close to his chest, and whispered the rest of the lyrics, hoping that he would dream himself home again to Jolmy and the village.

3

A FULL BLADDER awoke Adam. Panicked in his blindness, he thrashed around, disoriented, not knowing where he was or how he got there.

Then he remembered. A giant mongoose had chased him through a gate in a tunnel, after he had escaped a kidnapping attempt by shrinking and running into a rat hole.

What?

Had he gone insane?

He didn't feel insane. And yet ...

The dirt floor was real. The dirt walls were real. The metal on the mysterious gate was real. The cards in his pocket were real. At least they all seemed real. But dreams also feel real.

How would he know if this was a dream or not?

Occam's Razor. The simplest answer was likely the right answer.

Then this had to be a dream.

He reached up and ran his hands around the metal gate. How could there be a functional metal gate, complete with locking mechanism, in a rat tunnel?

He stood up, running his hands along the wall until he found what seemed to be a corner, and urinated loudly. When finished, he walked to the opposite corner and sat down. He scrubbed his fuzzy teeth with his shirttail, and wished for a cool drink of water to quench what was a growing thirst. Food was going to be an issue, but water was going to be an issue first. His tongue was already sticky. And he was hot. Sweating. Losing even more water through perspiration.

The slow surge of panic began to build. His heart raced, perspiration beaded out on his forehead, a metallic taste formed on the back of his tongue.

He had to find something to drink.

Panic would not help. To calm himself, Adam closed his eyes and thought of the village, somewhere above him, where, before the Justice Corps came in, the women walked over a mile every day, fetching enough river water to sustain their families. He could last a little longer without water. He would have to find it, of course, but he wasn't desperate yet.

Yet.

He consciously willed himself to calm down. He would find water. He would get out of this. Or he would wake up. Sometimes the best thing is just to wake up, and this could be one of those times.

The lump on the side of his head had gotten smaller. The pounding headache had been replaced by a dull, constant pain that he was certain could be vanquished by a long drink of cool water.

Heart again calmed, blood pressure back to normal, he pulled the deck of cards from his pocket and shuffled through them. He couldn't see anything in the dark, but they clearly held some kind of magical powers.

He passed a finger over each one individually, as if he could divine what its powers were by feel. The first one had shrunk him to the size of a rodent. The second one had created a doorway he could escape through.

Was that true? Had the card created the doorway? The gate?

Did the cards know what he needed at the moment and provide it, or had he been extremely lucky? What if the card he threw at the mongoose had shrunk him further? He might have been stepped on and squashed.

Adam ran his hands across his face. He couldn't sit here much longer. He had to do something. He wished he knew how long he had been unconscious in captivity. He wished he knew how long he'd been sleeping. He wished he knew how far had he been driven to his prison cell from the road to the village.

His beard seemed to be about three days old.

Three days!

If he could somehow orient himself, he would know which tunnel to take in order to get back to the village.

He barked a bitter laugh that deadened in the earthen room. There was no way for him to orient himself. It didn't seem to make much sense to get underneath the village if he couldn't get up to the village and the sunshine and all his friends, but at least it was a goal.

He had to go somewhere.

Actually, it might be better to go back to the prison cell. At his current diminutive stature, he could probably get out of the cell unnoticed by the guards, or thugs, or rebels, or whatever they were.

He visualized sneaking back out of the rat hole into the cell. When someone opened the door, he would slip past them out into the hot, steamy jungle, and somehow get into one of the vehicles. Then maybe he could throw a magic card and return to normal size.

As ludicrous as that sounded, it actually seemed to be the best plan. Maybe he could even get his Jeep back.

It might be a stupid plan, but at least it was a plan.

He stood and ran his hands over the bars of the gate. No latch.

He pulled and pushed, trying to rattle the gate, or dislodge it from its earthen anchor, but it was as solid as if it had been forged out of bedrock. It appeared as if going back to his prison cell was not an option.

Maybe he could throw a card and get it unlocked. Even if the cards were precious, they could be used, and each one produced a burst of light by which he could see and get his bearings.

He pulled a card at random from the pack, then put the pack back into his pocket.

Flipping the corner with his finger, he prayed to not only his God, but to the god of the cards.

"I need water," he whispered. "I need to get home. I need food. I need direction."

Emotion surged behind his eyes, clogged his throat. He paused for a moment. Then, voice cracking, "I need help."

He stood up and prepared to flick the card at the wall.

Wait a minute.

Maybe he ought to be very specific about what he needed. Maybe the cards did whatever they were going to do regardless of his wishes or prayers, or needs, but then again, maybe they bent to his will.

"I need water," he said, and flicked the card at the wall.

The familiar concussion boomed, punching him in the chest, popping his ears, and bands of blue light radiated out.

Adam looked around quickly, trying to see everything he could in that brief, blinding flash.

He saw something reflect, something winked from way down the tunnel he was in. There was something down there, perhaps something metal.

He gave the gate bars another shake.

Solid.

Abandoning the idea of getting back out through the gate and escaping through the prison cell, instead he walked toward where he thought he saw the glinting object. The tunnel led downhill, deeper into the underground. He walked carefully, keeping the vision of the glinting item and its location firmly in his mind's eye. He wanted to walk directly to the reflecting object and see what it was. He hoped it was a digging tool of some sort, no matter how preposterous that thought seemed to be.

Could he tunnel through the ceiling, straight up into the sunshine?

Why not?

The ground was strewn with detritus that he kicked as he walked. He had to be careful not to trip as he approached the place where he was certain he saw something metallic.

When he stepped on it, he knew. It crinkled beneath his foot. He got down on all fours and examined it. Straight line on one side, serrated on the other side.

He smelled it.

Juicy Fruit.

A foil gum wrapper. Almost big enough to serve him as a kind of space blanket. It was something. Something useful. But there were other things here, too.

He folded the wrapper as best he could and tucked it into his waistband. Then, crawling on all fours, he examined the pile of junk.

He climbed over piles of sticks and found round things that seemed to be made of cardboard. A bottle cap, shredded pieces of plastic, and rope.

He pulled on the rope. It was buried in the pile of trash, wound around things, but the more he pulled on it, the more pleased he was to see that there was real length to it. It was probably just a piece of string, but to him, it was rope. He coiled the rope and put it over his head and one arm so it lay diagonally across his chest.

There were many big, soft log-shaped things, and it took him a moment to realize they were likely rat droppings. Fresh rat droppings.

Were dried rat droppings flammable? In Africa, animal dung was commonly used as fuel. Could he make a fire with rat droppings, and maybe some of the pieces of paper he had found?

What would he do with a fire?

He could make a torch. He could cook food, if he had any.

Were there roots coming through the sides or roof of this place that he could cook and eat? How would he find them? How would he cook them?

He needed light. He could only do so much in absolute darkness.

Adam sat down and wrapped the foil around his shoulders. That was comforting in a weird, Juicy Fruit way. He patted his shirt pocket, a habit he had never lost since he quit smoking when his first daughter was born, over fifteen years ago. Still, when he relaxed, or found himself stressed out, he touched that breast pocket where he had always kept his cigarettes.

There was something in it.

He opened the button and put a finger inside.

Then he remembered. It was a photograph of Chrissie and the girls. He took their photo when they first arrived. He'd had that first photo printed, and carried it in his shirt pocket.

The Swan Girls. The card was approximately the same size as the magic cards.

Strange, how cards were now saving his life in this bizarre twist of the supernatural, and he had been carrying one with his own personal goddesses on it all this time. It was now his Goddess Card.

He ran his thumb over it, then touched it to his cheek, hoped his goddesses had arrived home in Minnesota safely. He kissed the photograph, and put it back in his breast pocket, buttoning it securely inside. If he should die down here, some day some hydrologist laying water line might dig up his tiny little bones and find a tiny little picture in his tiny little shirt pocket.

He pulled the remaining cards from his other pocket and went through them one by one. They were thicker than normal playing cards. He knew the feel of the usual playing cards by touch, as he and the other men of the village played cards almost every night before Chrissie and the girls came. That was how he bonded with the local men on his water crew. They played cards in the gloaming after dinner, smoked, drank, and laughed.

Homesickness nicked him. He missed those guys.

Did they miss him? Were they looking for him? Worse, had they notified Chrissie that he'd gone missing?

Nothing he could do about that now. "Accept the things I cannot change," he whispered.

Back to the cards. These cards were bigger in size, and the card stock weightier than the ones he played with in the evenings.

He wished he could see them.

He turned them over one by one. "I need light," he said out loud. One by one, he flipped them over onto his thigh, not knowing what else to do. "I need light," he said and flipped a card. "I need light."

Then one of the cards had a different attitude. Heavier. Like it had potential.

He stacked the rest of the cards and buttoned them into his shirt pocket with the photo of his girls.

"I need light," he said, bracing himself against the shockwave he hoped would come, and flipped the card at the wall opposite him.

The shockwaves emanated as usual, the pulse knocking him back against the wall, and illuminating, for a moment, the enormous pile of junk in the rat's nest.

Then the flash of light was gone, but on the ground directly in front of him, a little blue flame burned all on its own.

Adam blinked his eyes, not certain if he was actually seeing it, or if he was still blinded by the flash.

The little flame illuminated a circle around it. Dirt. Dirt floor.

He put his hands toward it.

No warmth.

He held out the end of his rope and teased it into the flame, but it did not burn.

This was a magic flame. He didn't know what properties it had, nor how long it would last, so he had to make good use of it while he could.

Gently, he reached over and picked it up between two fingers, then set it on the palm of his hand. It burned a bright blue. Held up, it illuminated a far greater area than it had on the ground.

Light! He had light.

Carefully, Adam got to his feet. He held the flame up high.

The rat's nest stretched for what seemed like miles down into the darkness. Surely there would be some great treasures to be found in there, but he didn't want to linger, nor did he want to climb over the huge pile of crap that likely led to a dead end.

Not to mention: this rat would be back.

Adam doubted there was anything in the rat's nest to eat or drink, and short of getting the hell out of there, those were his immediate needs.

He refolded the foil blanket, tucked it into the waistband of his pants, and then walked back to the gate.

The gate was still there. Shiny brass bars still firmly closed.

He rattled it anyway, or tried to rattle it, but it held firm. Firm like a weird, latchless magic gate in a rat hole would be.

There had to be another way.

Holding the flame high, he saw that there was a smaller tunnel that led away from the gate, away from the rat's nest. It led away from the prison, and it might even lead closer to the village.

Adam took a deep breath, wiped sweat from his face, held his blue flame up high and walked with what he hoped was confidence-building purpose.

The tunnel turned immediately to the right, and began a decidedly downward slant.

Adam tried to quiet his pounding heart and descended further into the dark underworld, illuminated only by the small circle of blue light.

4

ADAM WALKED UNTIL he was out of breath. Desperate to get somewhere, anywhere, before the comforting blue light extinguished, he walked as quickly as possible over the uneven terrain. Continually tripped up by roots, rocks, and the occasional shard of old pottery and long-buried bits of glass and plastic, he kept marching relentlessly forward, ever farther down the tunnel.

Down was not the direction he was interested in going, but there was no other way, unless he turned around, walked back uphill, and then slogged through the rat's nest.

Don't second guess yourself. You made a commitment. Now just go with it.

Perspiration dripped off his nose and chin, and the headache was back, pounding with every footfall.

He picked up one triangular-shaped shard of glass that had a point and an edge to it, and put it in his pocket.

Smaller tributary tunnels branched off, but they were small and low, and Adam wasn't certain they led anywhere that would benefit him.

Thick roots were of particular annoyance, but he got used to climbing over them. He could set the flame down and use both hands if necessary.

Thirst was a growing problem. His tongue had grown thick and furred, and the longer he walked, the more he stumbled. The thought of water consumed him.

He slowed down and held the light up, looking at the wall of the tunnel for a root that would provide some moisture and perhaps even some nutrition.

This was a well-traveled tunnel—traveled by many somethings over a long period of time, and anything that looked promising had been gnawed off at the wall, the ends dried to nothing. If he was going to find anything to eat, he would have to dig it out.

He began digging at a promising looking root with the bit of glass he had picked up—as if he knew what a promising root looked like. It certainly didn't look like any carrot or potato he had ever eaten.

He wished he had paid more attention when Chrissie started the kitchen garden. He had provided the muscle for building the raised beds and hauling compost. He certainly enjoyed eating the bounty, but he did none of the actual gardening, and therefore had learned nothing.

He couldn't identify a nutritious plant from a weed if his life depended upon it.

And here he was, his life depending on it.

Lots of weeds were nutritious, he knew, but were the roots? Dandelion greens were edible, but their roots were poisonous. Rhubarb stalks were edible, but their leaves were poisonous.

Those were two facts he knew because he was a father. Beyond that, how would he know what was poisonous?

If he got sick and died, that's how.

The side wall of the tunnel had grown hard-packed over time, and the root he was digging seemed less and less likely, so he gave up on it. The effort only took time, made him hotter and thirstier.

He put the piece of glass back into his pocket and carried on, walking, stumbling, holding the blue flame ahead of him to provide companionship and reassurance as much as anything else.

The toe of his shoe caught on a rock embedded in the pathway, and he went down hard. His glasses flew from his face, the cards spilled out of his unbuttoned pocket, the flame, with its limited blue aura, landed far down the tunnel, leaving him in the dark.

He scrambled around, searching desperately for his glasses. He found them. They were bent, but not broken. He assembled the cards into a deck, but wasn't certain that he had them all. The deck was quite a bit smaller, but unwilling to crawl around in the dark looking for more, he just put what he had back in his pocket and buttoned it, this time, for safekeeping.

It would be easy to just use one for water, wouldn't it? Wish for water and fling a card, and maybe water would appear.

But which card?

Adam got to his feet, dusted himself off, found a hole in the knee of his pants and hoped he wasn't bleeding.

He walked down to the blue light and sat on the hard ground to catch his breath.

He examined his knee, found a scrape, but no blood to speak off. He set the flame on his other knee and pulled the cards again from his pocket.

This was not like any deck of cards he had ever seen before. Each card was different. Each one was beautifully illustrated in black and white, but gave no indication as to what magic it held, or represented, or would produce. He shuffled through them again and again, looking for one that might mean water, or escape, or food. But what he found was the stuff of Jormy's superstitions: Kings, Queens, Knights, Pages.

Would throwing a King card bring forth Jormy's King of the underworld? Would a Queen take pity on him?

Not likely.

He kept looking through the cards. The Moon, The Devil, Death.

He put those last two back in his pocket. He didn't know what they did, but he didn't want to find out. King of Cups, King of Swords, The Hanged Man, The Tower, Holy Water—

Wait. Holy Water. Perhaps that would be the one. And Cups. Queen of Cups and Holy Water. Would one of those get him a cup of water?

It seemed too simplistic, it seemed too silly, but what else could he do?

He held the two cards in his hand, fingering the corners. He'd been incredibly lucky so far.

But really, now, did he want a cup of water, or did he want to get the hell out of here?

He set those cards aside and went back to the deck. Which card was most likely to get him back to the surface? Back to the village? Back home?

The Sun. There was a card with a sun on it and what looked like a field of sunflowers. That was what he needed. He needed the sun, he needed flowers. He needed to be above ground. He put the Queen of Cups and the Holy Water cards back into his pocket and held up the Sun card.

He paused. Didn't Jolmy say that the underworld king of gods or whatever ruled the sun and the moon? And stars?

There was a moon card. And a star card.

This can't be happening.

"I need to be out of here," he whispered, then thought if he was going to ask favors of magic, he ought to be very,

very specific. If it worked, he needed it to work correctly. This was not a time to be sloppy or to be careless with his word choice.

He held up the Sun card. "I wish to be above ground," he said. He shielded the blue flame from the anticipated shockwave and flicked the card at the wall.

The now-familiar rings of light blasted forth and then faded.

Nothing. He was still here, five inches tall, stuck in a rat tunnel. Thirsty, hungry, lonely, scared.

Dying.

He took a deep, disappointed breath and leaned back against the wall. He set the flame on the ground next to him, unfolded his foil blanket, wrapped it around him, and closed his eyes.

Maybe he could sleep for a little while and when he awoke, the magic he had summoned would have had time to work. Maybe it wasn't always as instantaneous as he imagined, or as he demanded.

He let his head fall back to rest on the dirt wall and tried not to think about water. Instead, he thought about praying again, but that was an activity that seemed more appropriate above ground, where everything made sense. How could God make one set of rules for the daylight, society, life and families, and another set of rules for the underworld?

Jolmy knew.

Jolmy had been far more willing to incorporate Adam's Christian god into his life than Adam had been willing to incorporate Jolmy's.

He had much to learn.

Adam curled up and closed his eyes.

He dreamed of his girls. He dreamed of pushing the littlest one, Mouse, in a swing. It was a beautiful sunny day, blue sky, puffy clouds. The other two girls were playing next to a stream, and Chrissie was laying out a picnic lunch on a red checked tablecloth.

She pulled a big, frosty bottle of water from the basket. Adam could see each droplet of condensation sliding down. He walked toward it, suddenly thirsty beyond all reason.

"Daddy!" Mouse called. "Daddy!"

But he ignored her, walking directly to his beautiful wife and that cool, delicious water. He only had eyes for the water. His tongue licked parched lips as he imagined tasting that cool water, feeling it slide down his throat and hit his hot belly with a wondrous splash.

Halfway to it, thunder rolled.

He looked back toward Mouse, still in the swing, only now she was screaming: "Daddy!"

He couldn't see what was causing thunder; the sky was clear blue.

Mouse was pointing now and shouting at him. He turned, and a black moving blanket, a living, undulating horde covered the ground, a billion feet thundering toward him and his family.

"Run!" he shouted at his wife, who smiled up at him, oblivious.

"Run!"

Adam startled awake. The thunder was real. It was coming from his left, straight down the tunnel.

He picked up the blue flame that had begun to sputter, and abandoning his gum wrapper blanket, he hurried down the tunnel, away from whatever monstrous thing was roaring toward him.

The thundering approached Adam with astonishing speed. He began to trot, and then to run, full out, as the sound got closer and closer. In the midst of his raspy breathing, he realized that it wasn't thunder at all, but footfalls. Hundreds and millions of feet pounding the ground. He had no idea what multitudes approached, but he didn't care much to find out.

Lungs burning with exhaustion, limbs weak with dehydration, he fumbled in his pocket for a card. Any card. He grabbed one and without looking at it, stopped and stood his ground. The last time he flung a card, he had wished for a way out. Instead, he got thundering hordes. This magic was unpredictable. It seemed as though he had it figured out at one point, but this latest showed that he had no idea. Worst of all, he was racking up magic debt every time he used one of the cards. Who knew what payback would be?

The pounding of feet shook the ground beneath him. Again, he shielded the faint, flickering blue flame. "I need to not be trampled," he whispered. He thought about that. No, that's not right. *I need to get out of here.*

Whatever it was, was almost upon him. Their stench was already upon him.

Hurry! Make a decision!

"Show me the way out!" he yelled, and flicked a card down the tunnel into the darkness. In the explosive shockwave that followed, he saw what was nearly upon him: Army ants.

The tunnel was filled with African ants with their giant red heads, their jagged mandibles, marching on the ground, the walls, the ceiling, many of them carrying white larvae, others carrying leaves and other detritus. He must have stumbled into some kind of an ant mound.

They were approaching with astonishing speed, and they were right in front of him, ready to trample him in their single-minded rush to wherever they were going.

Adam shielded his face with his arms, ready to be torn to pieces.

But the magic worked. In the flash of a moment, the stinking mass of ants vanished, and in its place was an ornate brass elevator, sitting calmly, its doors open and inviting.

What?

Adam blinked at it in disbelief.

This had to be a dream. Either that, or he really had gone completely insane.

One moment he was about to be trampled or torn to pieces by a horde of Army ants, and the next second they were gone and he was invited to step into an antique brass elevator.

All while he was trapped inside a rat tunnel.

He rubbed his hands over his face, over his eyes.

That had seemed to be such a close call. Those ants would have overcome him and ripped him to pieces in seconds. They would have devoured him.

Waning adrenaline sapped the last of his energy and he fell to the ground in gratitude that he hadn't been eaten by insects. Instead of chattering serrated mandibles, in front of him yawned the door of an old style brass elevator, red carpet, mirrored walls, and all.

This is not the dream of a sane man.

He sat quietly, watching to see if the elevator did anything odd, other than just appearing. It did not. He wished he still had his space blanket, but it had been abandoned. All that he had was the string/rope, the photo of his girls, a piece of glass, and the cards.

Traditionally, elevators went up and down. Perhaps this one would take him up.

The little blue flame he still carried sputtered and went out, but Adam was not left in the dark.

The elevator had its own faint, indistinct light source.

With great effort, he got to his feet, and stepped inside. The control panel was hidden by the double doors, the first of which was scissored.

He pulled it closed.

Automatically, the outer doors closed, and by the time he saw that this elevator only went down, it was too late to stop it. The metal box dropped into a stomach-lurching freefall. He waved his arms in a futile effort to keep his balance. Still, the car went down. Every second it went down, his hopes of ever seeing the sun again fell as well.

Eventually, he fell to the ground as the car's descent slowed and he tried to find comfort in the feel of actual carpeting underneath him.

The car shuddered to a stop.

Adam sat up and stared at the door. He didn't want to open it. He didn't want any of this. He wanted to be home in Minnesota with his wife and daughters, making breakfast in the morning and helping them get ready for school. He wanted to go to work as a normal person, wearing a shirt and tie, and drinking terrible office coffee and joking with the others in the engineering firm. He wanted to be up above ground in the village with his Congolese family and his Justice Corps family. He wanted to laugh with Jolmy and the crew, he wanted to hear them sing as they worked, he wanted to eat Belvina's delicious yam and rice dinners.

He did not want to be five inches tall, stuck in an impossible elevator deeply under the ground.

But sitting and wishing was going to get him nowhere. He needed water, he needed food, he needed to get out of here. Slowly, achingly, he stood up, grabbed the handle and pulled back the inner door. Then he backed away, not having any idea at all what might be on the other side of the outer doors.

They opened.

Blackness.

"Hello?" His voice echoed in an enormous room. He was no longer in a tunnel, he was in some type of a cave. Well, sometimes caves had water. He patted his breast pocket, sent love and affection to the photo of his wife and daughters, appreciated the comfort of the remaining weird cards, and stepped out of the elevator.

The light from the elevator winked out. He turned around, but all that was behind him was blackness.

No elevator, no light.

He shouted into the darkness. "Hello?" then listened to his voice echo.

He ran his hands over the wall. Smooth rock, as if it had been carved, worn, or chiseled out of stone. By hands or by water? This was not unlike water-carved caverns he had known in his past.

Water. The very thought of it made him weak. He held his head up and sniffed the air. Dank. There was definitely water somewhere near. If only he had more light. Dare he spend another card on the possibility of either water or light?

Why not?

He had fuckall to lose.

He pulled a card at random from his pocket and threw it at the wall. The circles of shockwave illuminated only the immediate environs, but what he did see was a giant pit, and it was mere steps from his feet. Had he taken two steps, he would have fallen to his death.

But did he get water? No.

Did he get light? No.

The magic wasn't working, at least it wasn't working in the way he needed it to work.

But wait.

What was that sound?

He doubted even his own sanity at this point, so of course he doubted all his senses. Slowly, as if the sound was emerging, coming into focus, he heard water.

It sounded like a little stream, tiny splashes over rocks, teeny waves against a shore, little drips from hanging mosses.

He got down on his knees and approached the edge of the pit. Slowly, testing the integrity of the edge, he put his face over the abyss and listened. Yes! Definitely water.

His thirst blossomed into a desperate need.

It could be just a mirage. An auditory hallucination. It could be magic water. It could be harmful. It could be acid.

He had to get down to the source. All he had was the rope he carried across his torso. He closed his eyes and tried to envision the size and scope of the pit from the brief flash of the card concussion, but it was so brief—and he hadn't looked down to see how far down the water was. He needed something to tie the rope to, then he could rappel down to the water.

Who was he kidding? He was no athlete. His upper body strength had left him right after high school basketball. He was a scholar, not a climber. An engineer, not a gym rat. How the hell could he rappel down a rope?

Not only that, but he didn't know if the pit was deeper than his rope was long. And what was the situation with the water below? Was it a raging river that would sweep him deeper underground? Or would it flow gently out above ground in a nice river, or stream, where he could actually see the sun and the sky, and swim for shore?

He had no choice. On hands and knees, he crawled the perimeter of the pit until he found a rock outcropping that seemed solid enough to hold his weight. He tied one end of his rope around the rock, and as he knelt to tie handhold knots in the line, the dirt edge crumbled and gave way.

He slid into the abyss.

He clung to the rope, but his grip was no match for his weight on the steep decline.

He dug his heels into thick moss to try to slow his descent, but it didn't help. The moss just scraped off the smooth rock.

The rope quickly burned his palms, and then it was gone, and still he slid, arms and legs out wide, holding his head up so it wouldn't be beaten on the rocks, trying not to tumble, trying desperately not to start rolling.

Down and down, faster, and faster, until the slope ended, and he went airborne, as if off a ski jump.

He flailed in the complete darkness, not even knowing for certain which way was up.

And then he was in the water. Deep, cold water. He thrashed about, kicking and swimming as fast as he could to get back to the surface, but the water was deep, deeper than he expected, and the current strong.

When he broke the surface, he took great gulping breaths of air, and then he took huge swallows of cool water. It slid across his tongue and down his throat as smoothly and sweetly as any water he had ever tasted.

This was not the ice cold water of Minnesota, but it was cool on his overheated body. He splashed around deliriously, paying little attention at first to the fact that he was headed downstream, and headed downstream fast.

He maneuvered himself so that he was going down feet first. That way, if there was a rock, he would hit it with his feet and not his head. Minnesota River Rafting 101. He arched his back and let the river take him, floating lightly and fairly effortlessly along.

The hydrologist in him knew that this water was leading most likely to a lake, or a bigger river. Even if it stayed underground for miles, eventually it would merge with other waters and spill into the ocean.

The village was a long way from any ocean, but there were myriad lakes and rivers, and any one of them would do.

With any luck ...

He busied himself with floating, staying horizontal in the underground stream, head up and out of the water, moving feet first in total blackness, ready for the next change.

This river wasn't going to stay underground forever.

He didn't wait long. The water sped up as the cavern the water flowed through began to narrow.

The walls closed in, and he could hear his breath on the ceiling of the cavern. He sped along like a bullet in a rifle barrel.

Within moments, the passage would likely narrow further, and he would be underwater. Perhaps it would narrow to the point that he couldn't fit. He could get stuck. There would be no going back, not against this current.

The taste of panic on the back of his tongue returned.

He gulped great breaths in anticipation—each breath could be his last—but the river carried him along with just enough room for his face to surface and take a breath. He tried to slow his progression by walking his hands along the ceiling of the cavern, feeling the water tug on his clothing, the waistband of his pants, his shoes.

He listened carefully, in case the cavern opened up on one side or another and he could crawl out for a rest, but so far, the river just kept on sweeping him down through the small tunnel in the pitch dark, to parts unknown.

Something hit him in the face, ripped off his glasses, and when he reached for it, he found it to be a root, sucking moisture from the river. There were many. He grasped at them with hands blistered and burned from their slide down the rope, and held on. He hooked his arm through a loop of root as the river pulled him relentlessly forward.

The current pulled hard on him, and the root gave a little bit.

The rushing water sucked off a shoe.

Then the river pulled off his other shoe, and he was in danger of losing his pants.

He hitched up his waistband with his free hand and crossed his legs as best he could, while fumbling in his breast pocket for another card.

The current ripped a few cards from his hand and he held on to the others with desperation.

The deck was dwindling fast.

That didn't matter. He either had enough cards or he didn't. He either had enough magic or he didn't.

Perhaps this time the Knave of Coins would bless him with a boat for this river. Adam barked out a quick laugh. This could be the River Styx, taking him straight to Hell.

"I need to be above ground," he said, and flicked the card into the river. The familiar concentric circles blew him off his handhold, and he sailed on down the waterway.

He grabbed onto his belt, saving his pants, and on his chest burned the soft blue light.

It was back! And it seemed to be waterproof.

Magic was pretty cool, after all.

"Hello, old friend," he said, and desperately worked his arms to keep himself upright and cruising down the river feet first.

The river shot him into a tunnel so small again he feared he would get stuck.

His hands scraped rock on all sides, and the current pulled on him, harder, relentlessly. He took a last gasp of air and stretched out his arms and legs and tried to make himself as thin as possible.

He went right through the tube and out the other side.

The current slowed.

He bobbed to the surface, and though he couldn't see much by the light of the blue flame that stuck to his shirt, he could tell he had come out into a big cavern.

The river had emptied into a great underground lake.

Adam took a moment to take a couple of deep breaths and calm his heart. That had been one crazy ride in absolute darkness. But hydrated and moving was better than dehydrated and stuck in a hot dirt tunnel.

"Hey!" he shouted. His voice echoed off the ceiling, far above his head.

The cavern wall on the left seemed far away but not so far on the right.

"Hello!" he called, and the sound of his voice bounced right back from the right.

Waves lapped on the shore.

Slowly, holding the flame above the water, he swam long, slow strokes toward the shore. His stocking feet touched a pebbly bottom.

Not having shoes was going to be a real problem.

He put the flame on his shoulder and a healing warmth begin to work on the knot on his head. Perhaps the flame was not only a light, but also a healing magic. He could use a little of that as well. He climbed out of the water and onto a rocky shore, strewn with what looked like small pieces of driftwood, smoothed off by years of water wear. There was other junk, too, old ripped-up plastic bottles, fishing nets, a mailbox big enough for him to live in, the remnants of a paperback book, all manner of crap that civilization had created.

This was the first normal thing he had seen since this whole weird adventure started.

It would be nice if he found a pair of teenie shoes amidst the debris.

Where the tunnels had been hot and steamy, this cavern was huge, open and cold. He sat down, shivering, and caught his breath, sending prayers of thanks to God above.

Prayers seemed hollow and useless in this place, though. The god of his understanding, the god of his belief, his Christian god, did not extend to magic and underworld craziness such as brass elevators in rat tunnels and heatless, waterproof blue flames that healed.

He had left his god back in the village, back in Africa, back in America, back in the sunshine. No gods existed down here, except maybe Jolmy's god of the underworld. And Adam had no idea how to pray to that type of deity.

So for now, he rested, fresh water sloshing in his belly, looked around and sifted through the junk that was all around him. If he moved around, got his muscles working, he would warm up.

He held the flame up and looked deeper on both sides of the shore.

From what he could tell, he'd been washed ashore like the acres of trash he could see, and there was much more that he couldn't see. Trash, as far as the light extended his vision, and in piles much taller than he.

Slowly, carefully, he picked his way through, looking for a tiny, undamaged bottle that he could use to carry fresh water with him.

But not only were the ones he found damaged, they were as big as he was.

Something that looked a lot like a coconut—and he had seen plenty of them since being in the jungle—lay half buried in rocks and sticks.

Of course a coconut could wash down that river and float its way to the shore, especially during the rainy season.

Adam crawled over to it, climbing over the mounds of debris, careful about his skinned knee, careful about being only in stocking feet.

Indeed it was a coconut, but they were hard to open. At his size, that would be nearly impossible. The thing was the size of a car.

The local people at the village knew how to open a coconut. In the center of the village they had a metal stake buried deeply into the ground, and they shucked the outer shell of a coconut in no time by hitting it on that stake. The fibers were so tough that the women wove floor mats with them, twisting them into ropes.

Fibers into ropes.

No, he had no time for that. Opening the coconut was out of the question, and he had no time to pull fibers and twist them into ropes long enough to be of any use.

But if a coconut had washed down, perhaps other food had as well.

Adam set the blue flame on top of the coconut and began digging through the sticks and vegetation that had piled up on the shore. Dead fish. Rotten fruit. Waterlogged cardboard boxes.

His fingers touched something firm and round, and he dug through rocks and trash with renewed interest.

A gourd. Or a squash. Or something, as big as his head. Bigger. Soft, as if overripe, but it didn't seem to be rotten. It didn't smell rotten.

Suddenly, hunger overwhelmed him. The ache in his belly ignited a desperation for something to eat, something nutritious, not something dead or rotten.

This could be it.

With the shard of glass he had saved, he cut open the rind, stuck his hand inside and pulled out a fistful of fibrous meat with what looked like seeds still attached.

A pumpkin! Well, not a real pumpkin, but some kind of a squash nevertheless.

Soft and squishy, tart and more delicious than anything he had ever tasted, he ate the flesh. He cut open and ate the soft interior of the gigantic seeds, gorging himself, swallowing without even chewing, eating like a madman, until he could eat no more.

The very act of such a feeding frenzy left him exhausted.

He lay back next to the big coconut and tried to review what had happened to him. Tried to make sense of something so tremendously nonsensical.

He wanted to rest. He wanted to reflect. He wanted to have a moment's peace, but he had limited light, and limited time, and limited cards, and he was still stuck underground in the dark. He jangled, as if he should be doing something, up and rummaging around, looking for something useful to carry with him, or a way out that didn't include being washed through any more claustrophobic lava tubes, or whatever the hell that was.

He wanted to get back on the move, but his belly was full and his hands hurt. His muscles hurt. His head hurt. He desperately needed to rest.

Slowly, and with great deliberation, he touched his breast pocket, made sure it was buttoned securely over the cards, then he packed one giant squash seed in each of the cargo pockets in his pants, just in case they might come in handy later. He went to the edge of the water and washed the stickiness from his face and hands.

Clean, nourished, hydrated, still alive, and with the cool flame as his traveling companion, he wrestled a piece of cardboard from the debris, pulled it over him, curled up next to the giant coconut, and slept.

5

HE DREAMED of Jolmy.

Jolmy, his great Congolese friend who was the foreman on the village water project. A big, black man with a shy, sweet wife and four beautiful children, Jolmy was always happy, always grinning, always appreciative of the help from the Justice Corps volunteers who came to make his village an easier and better place to live.

Adam lived with Jolmy and his family until his own family came to visit for the summer. Adam slept on a mat on the floor of the open-walled living/dining/kitchen room. That's where the children usually slept, but as long as Adam was their guest, the kids slept with Jolmy and Belvina in their room. Adam was always surprised and touched by their attention to his privacy in a place where privacy barely existed.

When his family came, they were given their own little one-room house, built of scavenged scraps, but as soon as he put Chrissie and the girls on the plane, he would be back to his coconut-fiber mat on Jolmy's floor.

In Adam's dream, Jolmy's face loomed large. Above ground, his booming laugh could be heard all across the village, but now, down here in the labyrinth, his face was stern, his dark bloodshot eyes riveted directly on Adam's face. "You do not tease the gods of the underworld," he said. "They are not kind. You do your business and you get out. And you must always leave a sacrifice for them."

Sacrifice?

"The underground gods are angry and they are jealous. They covet you everything. They covet you youth, you whiteness, you clothes, you education. They will steal it all if they can, but if you leave them something, they might let you go. So leave them something you value so they don't take insult."

Something of value.

"If you don't leave them something, they will take something, something you prize."

Adam startled awake.

"Jolmy?" he called, but even as he opened his mouth, he remembered where he was and knew that Jolmy had come to him in a dream.

The comforting blue light began to sputter.

Jolmy had said that he had to dream himself out from the underground. Were his dreams something that he could use? How could one wield a dream?

And what on earth could he leave behind that would entertain, or at least placate these underground gods, of which he knew nothing? Were his shoes not enough? His glasses? His blood and sweat and fear—this wasn't enough?

Adam sat up, rubbing his face.

The blue light had diminished to a barely visible little pinprick, sitting atop the coconut where he had left it.

"Please don't go," he beseeched it, and as he did, it winked out.

Darkness again closed around him.

The vague sound of water lapping at the shore mixed with sharper sounds of some kind of night creatures sifting through the debris on shore. Crabs?

At his size, they might be big enough to ride.

Oh God, at his size, he would be just the right size for them to eat.

He remembered hearing that Amelia Earhart was likely eaten by crabs on the island where her plane crashed.

The thought had made him shudder at the time, but now it horrified him. The thought of being eaten by giant Army ants was nothing compared with the thought of being picked apart by crabs.

He leapt to his feet, and kept his feet moving, in case a crab got snagged on one of his socks, or tried to crawl up his pant leg.

He cursed himself for not making better use of the light while he had it. He could have looked for a way out of the cavern. He could have looked for his shoes. He could have investigated his surroundings.

Instead, he ate, and slept. But that was important, too. Imperative, even.

He reached into his breast pocket and pulled out the cards he had left.

They were waterlogged and swollen. Would they still work?

Magic doesn't care about a little waterlogging, does it?

He wanted shoes. He wanted light. He wanted to get the fuck OUT OF HERE!

He wanted to go home.

The tears he feared the underground gods required now overcame him. The sobs of exhaustion came freely, and proved to be a great emotional release. He felt stupid dancing in place to keep the crabs away, while crying, but there was no one to hear him or see him, there was no one for whom he had to put on a brave face. He could be small—more than literally—he could be vulnerable, he could be afraid, and it was all right.

The emotional storm didn't last long. He wiped his face, blew his nose, then washed his face and hands again at the edge of the lake.

"There," he said to anybody who was listening. "I've sacrificed blood, sweat *and* tears. Can I go home now?"

Unfortunately, he feared the only ones who heard him were the crabs and rats rooting through the stuff on the shore.

He sat cross legged and leaned against the coconut, hyper alert for the sound of any crustacean who dared to approach.

Perhaps the gods of the underground could be persuaded. Perhaps they had compassion, or pity. Perhaps they could influence the magic of the cards.

Adam counted the cards. He had sixteen left. Was that a lot? Would he need more?

It didn't matter. He had sixteen cards, and when they were gone, they were gone.

He took one, and put the rest of the deck back into his shirt pocket and buttoned it for security. He wouldn't be able to get to them in an emergency, but he wasn't likely to lose any by falling or being sucked down a river, either.

He sat quietly and calmed his mind, which was difficult, once he thought about the possibility of being eaten by the crabs that scuttled about. How big were they, compared to him? The size of dogs?

Again, he saw the little flickers of movement at the periphery of his vision. Little sparks.

He ignored them. Took a deep breath.

Calm.

Calm the mind.

The beautiful face of his fifteen-year-old daughter came clearly into his mind. She smiled at him with her light blue eyes and sandy hair. Lisa was the scholar of the family. She knew everything, and if there was anything she didn't know, she was on the internet finding out about it. A treasure trove of trivia, they all called her.

She would be starting her sophomore year in high school. She'd be getting her learner's permit and driving the old Volvo.

They say that it's not good to have a favorite child, but Adam, though he claimed not to, clearly did. Lisa had been their first. When he held that teenie, sweet-smelling newborn in his arms, he saw the faces of his mother, his grandmothers, his great-grandmothers, and surely all the women who had gone before. All their genes, all their DNA was represented in this tiny bundle of sweetness, wrapped up with the DNA of Chrissie, exhausted and sweaty, and never more beautiful.

From her earliest moments of talking, Lisa wanted to know everything. She sat in on all the adult conversations. She dreamed of going to college and getting multiple degrees, all before she was out of elementary school. At the moment, she had her heart set on Harvard Medical School. Adam and Chrissie would do everything they could to make that dream come true.

But if he died down here, Chrissie would never be able to manage that alone.

The familiar pang of guilt clenched his gut. Especially since … since he had "mismanaged" the girls' college funds.

He had to get out, if for nothing else than to make that right. He had to.

He lifted his face and his hands to the darkness of the cavern and the gods that were above it, beneath it, all around it.

"Thank you for the squash that nourished my body, and the water that sustains me," he whispered. "Thank you for the wild, mysterious magic that has saved my life from the rebel thugs. I am happy to pay you whatever you ask, but I ask you please to help me back to my village, back to my Congolese family, my Justice Corps family, and then to my American family in Minneapolis."

He ran his fingers around the edges of the card from his pocket. "I will pay whatever sacrifice you ask of me, if you will do this one thing for me."

He stood, took a deep breath and flicked the card at the wall of the cavern.

The concussion banged him in his chest with the blast of horizontal circles of light, and where he imagined the card hit the wall, a blue circle began to sizzle and grow, as if the light was melting a hole into the side of the cavern.

For a long moment, the cavern came to life, bathed in the thrilling light.

Adam looked around in amazement at the enormity of the cave, at the placid nature of the vast lake, at the piles of debris on all shores. Those piles could be mined for many things he could use, not the least of which was more food, and something of an appropriate size to carry water in. Maybe something for his feet. Sandals. Shoes, if he could find something that would fit his tiny size.

He looked around for an opening in the cavern, but saw none.

The only exit seemed to be the tunnel that the blue magic was burning into the rock.

That hole in the side of the cavern beckoned.

He could stay here, eat more squash, drink his fill of water. Rest. Try to get his flame back and search for his shoes.

He didn't want to rest. He didn't want to sleep where the crabs were likely to begin feasting on him.

He wanted to go home. He wanted to take Lisa to her driving test.

He stood up, looked around for anything he was leaving behind, but of course there was nothing, and he walked tenderly on stocking feet toward the entrance of the brand new tunnel.

The blue light continued chewing a hole in the rock, creating a long tunnel, leaving the faint smell of burned dirt behind. Adam stood in the darkening cavern as the light disappeared down the tunnel.

Yet another long, dark tunnel.

Was this the answer to his prayers? Or were the cruel gods of Jolmy's understanding toying with him? Would he find a way out, or was this just another in a long line of dead ends and other tortures?

He could always come back here to the water, the lake, the squash, the coconut. And since the lake had such a swift inlet, surely it had a swift outlet to match. He couldn't hear it, though, so likely it was underwater. He'd have to dive in total darkness, looking for it, feeling for the current.

Not an attractive option.

He looked back down the tunnel. The blue light was still working, only now it was way, far away, and as he watched, it turned a corner, leaving only the palest glow of blue reflected on the wall, very far away.

The rest of the cavern fell back into darkness.

Creatures again began scuttling around in the debris piles.

The tunnel invited him. If he ran, he could catch up to the blue light. He would be able to see, as long as he kept up with the crazy magical melting or digging of this tunnel through what appeared to be solid rock.

He had asked for this. He had engaged the magic, and now the magic was inviting him to engage with it.

Time to go.

He sat down, and with the help of his little piece of sharp glass, cut and ripped the sleeves off his shirt and wrapped each sleeve around the wet sock on each foot. It wouldn't be much protection for very long, but at least it would be some protection for a little while.

He stood up, picked his way across the rocky shoreline and stepped into the portal.

It smelled like fresh air.

Hope brought his spirits up. He thought he smelled the fresh African breezes that brought those dark blue clouds across the village and blessed them with rain squalls. When the rain came, all the children flew out of their houses to play in the water, to smear mud all over each other, to mud their hair and twist it into unnatural shapes.

The adults stood on the roofed porches and watched the children, smiling and recalling their youth. Jolmy would call a work stoppage and he would lean back in the chair on his own front porch and light up one of those stinky herbal cigarettes that he liked to roll and smoke.

Homesick for those sights and sounds, Adam started walking, and then he walked faster.

This tunnel, created by magic out of pure rock, was glassy and smooth to the touch. There were no rocks and roots to trip him up, nothing to stumble over. His feet were grateful, but walking with the sleeves tied around them became awkward and cumbersome. After a while, he untied the sleeves and saved them, tucked into his belt, in case the smoothness of the floor did not last.

He continued on in stocking feet. His wet, chafing clothes began to dry out in the heat of the tunnel.

At the end, the tunnel turned right. Way, far down, he could see the blue glow as the ring continued to dig well ahead of him. He began to jog.

The next turn was left.

He had to remember, in case the magic petered out and he needed to get back to the cavern, back to water and likely food. If he didn't fall prey to the creatures that skittered across the detritus, perhaps he would be big enough to kill and eat one.

Adam shivered at the thought of trying to kill a giant crab or rat as big as he was with his bare hands.

He wasn't that desperate. Not yet. He kept going, kept the glow of the blue light in his sight, and headed for it as quickly as he could.

But the tunnel-digging light was far faster than he, and soon he lost sight of it. Soon after, the glow of it winked out and he was alone again in the darkness. He slowed, walked carefully, hands windmilling in front of him and to the sides, so as not to run into anything.

The tunnel turned again left. It seemed as though he had merely done a u-turn and should soon be back to the cavern and the lake. Instead, he ran right into the end.

Dead end.

He ran his hands around both sides of the tunnel and the end. The sides of the tunnel were rounded, the floor and the end were flat. Smooth as glass. Seamless.

He shouted up at the ceiling in case the tunnel had inexplicably turned up, toward the surface, but the sound that bounced back clearly told him that he was at the dead end. Somehow, he had missed a turn.

How could he possibly have missed a turn?

Or, this was where the magic had just petered out. Like the little blue flame, it didn't last forever.

He backtracked, but the tunnel was too wide to touch both sides with his fingertips, so he kept up the windmilling rhythm. He began to sing, listening for a change in the sound of his breath as it echoed off the smooth black walls.

"Hey there, ho there, is anybody there ..."

There it was. A change in the echo of his voice, a turn to the right.

But the tunnel also kept going straight.

Now he had to make a decision.

If he turned to the right, was that the way he had come in? He didn't want to backtrack all the way back to the cavern, nor did he want to waste time and energy going down dead ends.

He stood for a moment, listening.

Silence. Deafening silence. Silence so complete he thought he heard things out of the corner of his ear, the way he continually saw flickers of movement out of the corner of his eye in the pitch blackness.

Silence so complete he thought he could hear his own insanity taking root and beginning to grow in the fertile soil of his paranoia.

The choice of one tunnel seemed to be the same as another.

He would go straight.

He began again working his exhausted arms, hoping that he wasn't going to fall into a pit while he was trying not to miss the next turn, or run nose-first into another dead end.

"Hey there, ho there …"

The echoes were very clear to his heightened sense of hearing. He knew when he was closer to the right side than the left side.

"Is anybody there …"

Okay, so from the cavern, he had turned left and left, but that was a dead end, so to get back to where he was, the way was really only one left and then a right. He didn't think he was either gaining or losing in elevation, so it was unlikely he was spiraling, he was just going straight ahead.

He detected another tunnel off to the right. A tributary?

Go right? Or straight ahead?

If he went right, he might merge with the tunnel that would take him back to the cavern. If he kept going, he might actually get some place.

Straight it is.

Sweating, muscles aching, socks worn through, feet blistering, Adam had to stop and rest.

The tunnel no longer smelled like a fresh rain squall, now it was back to smelling like burned dirt.

How could he have missed the way out to those fresh breezes?

God DAMN.

He sat down, back against the tunnel wall and worked with the shard of glass to open the hard coating of a giant squash seed from his pocket. It filled his hands, the size of a hamburger.

If he were normal-sized and on the surface of the earth, he would have traveled at least ten miles through these tunnels. Or so it seemed. But being a tenth of his usual size, it could be that he had only traveled a mile.

Should he continue?

How could he not continue?

And yet, his feet weren't going to be able to make it much farther. He could rewrap his feet in the sleeves from his shirt, but that wouldn't last long, either. Even though the tunnel floor was new and smooth, his feet were tender and unaccustomed to being without shoe leather.

What if he threw a card and wished himself normal size?

Well, he would never fit in this tunnel in that case. Would the tunnel grow with him?

Unlikely. Besides, he was not very good at getting what he wished for when he threw a card.

Still, he had options. He could continue to follow the tunnels, which now seemed more like an incomprehensible maze, or he could spend another card and see if it got him anywhere.

He finished eating the soft inner seed, wiped his sticky hands on his pants that were still damp from his slide down the river, unbuttoned his shirt pocket and took out the cards.

The last time he chose one in the dark, it had felt different. It was as if it had chosen him, instead of the other way around.

He weighed each card, but they all seemed to be the same. Nothing different. Maybe this was not the time nor the place to employ the magic. Maybe he was still supposed to follow the tunnel and just go where it led.

He closed his eyes and rested his legs, his feet, his hands, his brain.

"Is your heavenly god a trickster like our underground gods?" Jolmy's big face loomed in front of Adam.

He startled awake.

Jolmy wasn't there, of course, he was home with his family, while Adam was still stuck in the blackness of the tunnel. He had dreamed Jolmy. Jolmy and his trickster god.

Trickster! This was a trick. This had to be a trick of Jolmy's gods. But what was a trick? The tunnel? Or the cards? Was it all a trick and he would wake up in Jolmy's house, safe, happy, ready to get to work on finishing the water system?

No, somehow he had been tricked into this wretched place and was completely without resources to get himself out.

Well, he wasn't completely without resources. He was smart. He had a couple of gigantic seeds in his pockets. He had a bit of broken glass. And he had the cards, though they were dwindling. But for all the magic they had provided him, had he gotten any closer to home?

He didn't think so.

He was not a fan of Jolmy's gods. But then his traditional gods weren't helping much, either, were they?

He was no kind of pastor, not at all educated in the Bible or any other Christian works. He took his family to church now and then, but other than hearing the importance of being a good man and a good father, he didn't really pick up on much more.

Really? A good man? A good father?

When they asked him to teach Sunday school in the village, he was happy to do it. Missionaries had been here before, and many of the local residents knew more about the Bible than he did, but the little lessons appealed to everyone.

They loved the things like the Golden Rule. They delighted in happy things that weren't even in the Bible, like the Footprints in the Sand poem. The children all loved that, and he made up little quizzes for them, simple moral dilemmas that they would have to think about, ways to make it real to them. Being nice was always a good thing. Was a holy thing.

And here he was, in a definitely unholy situation.

One option he didn't have was to give up. He would not die in this tunnel. Not as long as he had stumps to walk on and a giant seed in his pocket. He would keep walking. He would navigate this maze in the darkness until he got home to his wife and daughters.

"Lisa," he whispered. "I'm coming home to you. Chrissie. Sonja. Mouse."

He stood on aching, trembling legs, got his balance on his raw feet and tried to remember if he had come from the left or the right.

No trickster god was going to keep him from his family.

In a burst of frustration, he pulled out a card and threw it at the wall. No wishes, no prayers. The gods knew what he needed, and maybe the magic did, too.

The concussion knocked him back against the wall, and he was horrified, in the flash of light, to see that there were many tunnels. Hundreds of tunnels, all leading off the tunnel he was standing in. Another identical tunnel every couple of feet. He was no longer in the main tunnel, whatever he thought that meant.

There were infinite choices, infinite possibilities for error, or death.

Were there also infinite possibilities for success?

When the flash ended, Adam saw that the little blue flame was back, burning brightly on the ground next to his foot.

He picked it up and a hot ball of emotion rose up his chest and lodged in his throat. He was so happy to have not only light, but the one thing that seemed to help him, the blue magical little companion that gave him hope.

"Welcome back," he said to it, and wiped his eyes. "Let's get out of here."

6

LISA FREQUENTLY REMINDED Adam of Occam's Razor. All things being equal, the simplest answer is likely the right answer. His eldest daughter was the scholar, writer, poet, and scientist in the family. Not especially interested in his field of fluid mechanics or hydrology beyond a basic knowledge, but she did believe in Occam's Razor from the very first time she heard it. She cited it frequently, at the breakfast table, in the car, on vacations, and whenever anybody else in the family was in the midst of a puzzling situation.

So if Occam's Razor was true, then Adam was dreaming. He was at home in bed in Minneapolis, dreaming of going to Congo with the Justice Corps and helping a village set up a water system. Or, he was already in Congo, mid-project, sleeping on a mat on Jolmy's floor.

Or maybe he was still a teenager, living in his parents' house, dreaming of his future.

Or maybe he was an old man, reflecting on what had been, what might have been.

Lisa, and maybe Occam, would say that he was caught up in a loopy nightmare.

And if that were true, then he could just sit down and bide his time until morning.

He reached up and probed the wound on his scalp where it had split open from the force of a baton in the hand of a revolutionary asshole.

Still tender. Wound closed into a long scab, lump still there, but much smaller. The scab was real. Definitely real. More real than any dream.

Even if it was a dream, it was not in his nature to just sit and wait to wake up.

He had to move.

He stood in the main tunnel, with myriad adjunct tunnels extending from it, like the teeth of a comb. "Which way?" he said out loud, as if the blue flame would answer him.

He held the light up high, looking for anomalies, anything that would sway his decision. But the tributary tunnels all seemed identical. All carved precisely—by the blue sizzling magic, he presumed—out of black rock. Every surface was the same, smooth and perfect as if melted from rock into glass. No ridges, no rivets, no edges, no flaws.

He could keep going forward in what he thought was the main tunnel, or he had an apparent infinite choice of side roads.

He kept going forward, along the main tunnel, the way he thought he was going before stopping to rest. He passed five, six, seven tunnel entrances, and then at the eighth, he paused.

Something was different here.

He listened.

Nothing.

He sniffed the air, but that wasn't it, either. He wet a finger and held it up, but there was no breeze, fresh or otherwise.

He sang into it. "Hey there, ho there."

His voice echoed as he expected it would. Close walls and ceiling, endlessly extending forward.

And yet, something was different. There was an alteration to the air, to the density of it. The other tunnels seemed dead, as if they were dead ends, or continued to wind around forever, but this one had something at the end of it.

Life.

He detected life.

With a deep breath, he headed into the tunnel, and to his amazement, it angled upward.

"Yes!" he said to the flame. "This is what we want. Closer to the surface. Ever closer to the sun, to the light, to grass and trees."

He continued to sing the song he had taught Lisa to sing whenever they were hiking in the woods. Minnesota bears didn't like being surprised by a silently marching family through their territory. So they sang, they sang loudly and in unison. "Hey there, ho there, hello you, bear there."

Good lord, he hoped the magic wasn't going to bring him a bear.

Despite being in fair to middling good shape, climbing a steep incline while singing took a toll, and Adam found that he needed to rest more and more frequently. Something at the end of this tunnel was calling him, but in that dreamish way, he couldn't quite get to it. The tunnel seemed to lengthen, as if he was walking in water, or sand. His salty, perspiration-soaked clothes again chafed his crotch, his neck, under his arms.

His blistered feet were numb. For that, he was grateful. The time would come when they would shriek at him.

This was all so very dreamlike.

He remembered childhood nightmares where he'd been kidnapped or tied up and thrown into the trunk of a car, but his mouth had somehow been befuddled and he could not scream. Or the dream when he was running from bad guys, but no matter how fast he ran, he made no headway and they gained on him, relentlessly getting closer.

Horrible nightmares. Invariably, he woke up panting, sweating, heart pounding. It took a long time—sometimes hours—for his body to calm down, for him to consider going back to sleep.

And now, here he was, stuck in a real nightmare.

Then, ahead, he saw a brightening. A faint light—*like daylight*—glistened off the side of the tunnel.

He set the blue flame on his shoulder again so he didn't have to carry it. He leaned forward and worked his screaming thigh and calf muscles up what now seemed to be a very steep ramp.

Daylight! Was it daylight? Could it be he was finally close to getting the hell out of here?

As he climbed, he tried to figure out where he was with respect to the makeshift prison cell, or with respect to the village.

There was no way he could know. If he came up in the middle of the jungle, hundreds of miles away from the village, that would be just fine with him. He would find a way home.

He would need to be normal size, of course, otherwise any one of a dozen jungle predators would make quick work of him.

But his size was a product of the underworld. Surely he would be a normal size when he got out of here.

And yet, he became this size while in the prison cell.

Adam shook these thoughts out of his head. It was better to think about being above ground, escaping this particular hell and getting home to the village.

If he came up in an area he didn't know, he could dodge into the jungle, or behind shrubbery or trees if he saw the rebel jeeps coming toward him. He could hitch-hike if he saw a farmer or a friendly face approach. It would be easy to get home, back to the village, he was sure of it, if only he was given the opportunity. If only he was above ground. If only he was back to his normal size.

He began to imagine the sun. The green plants. The soft earth. The raucous African wildlife. The unmistakable smell of the jungle, green and sweet, fetid and cloying, all at the same time. He imagined soaking his tortured feet in a cool stream. Hugging Jolmy and his wife and children. Being tended to by the village doctor. Telling the tale of his kidnapping. Regaling the village elders around the evening fire with his experiences of the trickster gods below.

He couldn't wait.

He very slowly made his way up the hill, leaning far forward, one laboriously slow step at a time, heart pounding, breath coming hard, his headache back, starting to hammer.

The light brightened as he neared. The tunnel turned to the left, and with each rasping breath raking his throat, his lungs aching with the effort, thighs and calves cramping, Adam reached the turn.

He stopped, hands on thighs, gasping for air. When he caught his breath, he stood up and made the turn.

He stood, stunned, in full light.

Ahead of him spread an incredible vista. It looked exactly like the countryside of Ireland. Rolling green hills, pastures separated by low rock walls. Little stone houses dotted the landscape, one-lane country roads wound between houses, streams gurgled through the pastures where sheep grazed. Each house had a picturesque little garden.

Ireland! What? *Ireland*?

But there was no blue sky. No clouds. Some indistinct light source illuminated the scene.

Not Ireland. He was clearly not yet above ground.

Another trick.

This had to be a mirage. This was evidence of his madness. He had been suspecting it for some miles now.

He wanted nothing more than to run down through the fields, to roll in the grass, to pull fresh clothes off the clotheslines and breathe deeply of their fresh scent. He ached to have a cup of tea in one of the kitchens with whatever portly, aproned woman cared to brew him one. He would eat her warm, freshly-baked scone, slathered with sweet butter and homemade jam. He was eager to pull up a fresh carrot or pluck a ripe, red, sweet tomato and smash it into his mouth.

But between him and the little path that led down into this dreamscape stood a sturdy gate with shining brass bars, exactly like the one that had separated him from that mongoose.

That was so, so long ago.

Softly, in the distance, a church bell tolled.

Adam gripped the bars on the gate and tried to rattle it.

Firm. Solid.

So near and yet so far.

His knees weakened in despair and he sank to the ground, hands gripping the bars like those on a jail cell, eyes feasting on that which he could not have, longing for that which he had taken for granted his entire life.

He closed his eyes and "Please, God!" escaped from his lips. He took a breath and opened his eyes.

It was still there. Tantalizing.

Tormenting.

Not real.

He looked at the archaic locking mechanism of the gate. There was no knob, no lever, no keyhole. He had no idea how to open it.

He gripped the bars with both hands.

"Hey!" he shouted. "Hey! Help me!"

His voice bounced back to him muffled. His plea didn't project down to the houses, to the little village beyond. He sounded as if he was shouting into a pillow-case.

Then a goose walked past the gate.

"Hey!" he shouted, but it did not pause, did not look at him.

Another followed it, and another, and soon there was a parade of geese, waddling single file past the gate.

Behind them came an old man with a tall walking stick, which he used to tend the geese and keep them going in a straight line. He wore a wool cap, heavy trousers, a shirt and jacket, and well worn heavy leather boots.

Adam almost forgot that he was small. This man was the same size as he. The geese proportional.

Had he grown back to a normal size in the tunnels?

No, a squash seed in his pocket was still the size of a sandwich.

"Hey," Adam said.

The man turned and looked at him.

"You can see me? Can you help me? Can you open this gate?"

The man frowned, removed his wool cap and scratched his bald head. "Don't know why I would want to do that," he said.

"Please," Adam said. "I'm hungry. I'm thirsty. I've been trapped in these—"

"There must be a reason for that," the man said.

"No!" Adam beseeched him. "No reason. I was kidnapped by thugs, and escaped into the tunnel, but now I can't get out of here."

The man looked at him, cocked his head as if considering Adam's plight. He put his hat back on and turned away.

"Let something in, let something out." The man shook his head, then walked on, tapping his geese into line.

Did he mean something essential from his idyllic little picturesque town would escape? Or that Adam would be a corrupting influence?

Or was there more to it?

"Please!" Adam shouted. "Help me! I don't belong here."

Adam put his arms through the gate and desperately searched for the latch. There had to be a way to open this gate, but even as he found no locking mechanism on the either side, he knew that the only way would be with magic.

He could throw a card.

But is this what he wanted? Did he want to be in this weird, sunless, underground village? Did he want to waste a card opening this gate and going into this town which might, in fact, just be a mirage?

Another trick?

He sat on the ground, leaning a shoulder against the cool metal of the gate and feasted his eyes at the pastoral scene.

He and Chrissie had honeymooned in Ireland. Lisa was likely conceived there. Here. No, not here, not in this crazy place that made no sense. His precious Lisa had been conceived in the *real* Ireland.

What was this beautiful, yet deceptive and unattainable Irish countryside doing in this nightmare of a dream? Was it to make him appreciative of all that he had at home?

He *was* appreciative.

Was it to remind him of something he had not done, or left undone, or something he needed to atone for?

None of it made sense.

He and Chrissie had stayed in a series of farmhouse B&B's, had driven the countryside, deliriously in love, drinking and eating with the locals in picturesque pubs, made love out in the open, made love in the farmhouses, made love in the rental car. It was a delicious honeymoon. Perfect in every way.

Except for that one thing.

Adam shook off that memory and gazed again on the landscape banquet laid before him.

He thought he even recognized this countryside. Thought he could see Mrs. O'Loughlin's sheets hanging on her clothesline.

Why would there be an identical replica of that here in this hellish labyrinth?

And who was the man with the geese? Was his presence—the only person Adam could see—significant somehow?

Or was it just more nonsensical nightmare stuff?

He wondered what he had looked like to the old man. Was that man walking along the base of a cliff face with dozens of brass gates set into it? Did each side tunnel off the main one end up here?

The man didn't seem surprised to see him. Had he seen others?

Had the town installed the gate to keep people like him from coming in?

He reached through the bars, stretched his arm as far as he could, and the whole landscape shuddered.

Wait. *What?*

He waved his hand and the landscape wavered.

He moved to the edge of the gate, put both hands through and felt around the ground, the sides, everything, as far as he could reach, straining, his face pushed hard into the bars of the gate.

Fabric. Something like canvas. He touched the edge, he moved it, and the entire village rippled like a flag.

This wasn't real at all. This scene had no depth. It was all an optical illusion. The town had been painted on a canvas with exquisite detail and perspective, and was hanging, apparently, just out of Adam's reach.

Still, smoke rose from chimneys. Water ran over rocks in the shallow stream. Mrs. O'Laughlin's sheets moved in the breeze. He had heard the church bell.

Had the old man been walking his geese between the canvas façade and the tunnel entrance?

Adam looked around for a rock to throw, or a stick to poke it with, but the smooth glass tunnel was barren. All he had was the little piece of glass and a couple of giant pumpkin seeds in his pockets.

In a moment of inspiration, he removed his belt, wrapped one end around his hand and stuck his hand again through the bars.

He flicked the buckle.

It hit the painting. The whole town wavered.

"Let something in, let something out," the old man had said.

What was behind that canvas stagecraft?

Adam got back to his feet, took a deep breath, trying to regain his pride after begging an old man for help. Disappointed beyond anything he had ever known before, he headed back down the ramp. He didn't even cast a final glance back at the false memory of Ireland.

Going down was harder on his feet than coming up, and by the time he made it to the main tunnel, the blue light was again sputtering, his calf muscles were screaming, and his bare feet were raw with blisters.

But he had a plan.

If this tunnel wasn't going to lead him out, surely the next tunnel would.

And if that tunnel didn't pan out, then he would try the next. And the next. And the next, until he got out of here. It would work.

He knew it with a fool's optimism.

It had to work. He was about out of options.

At the juncture, he turned left into the main tunnel, and the next tunnel entrance was barely six paces away, but the moment he turned into it, the blue light he carried on his shoulder winked out, and he had a very, very bad feeling in the pit of his stomach.

It wasn't just that he had been plunged back into darkness—he was getting used to that. This was more visceral.

This might be the end of the line for him. This was a place that swallowed hope. This was a place that told the truth, revealed ugliness, celebrated all the wrong things.

Chances are, he belonged here.

He could back out, choose another tunnel, but this one called to him. The opportunity to admit all his faults, all his wrongs, to be punished, or to have to pay for them in a meaningful way, was somehow, suddenly, very attractive.

Wait. Was it attractive because he was already in the tunnel? Should he back out and give this a second thought?

No. It didn't matter, because Adam knew immediately that this tunnel wasn't going to lead him to the fake little Irish town, or whatever was at the end of that other tunnel.

This tunnel wasn't going to lead him anywhere good.

And perhaps he deserved what he was about to get.

7

IT SEEMED TO ADAM that whatever evil dwelt in this tunnel hovered mere feet from him. Perhaps inches. On all sides.

He was surrounded by it.

He could smell its putrid breath.

An oppressive blackness encircled him. A thickening stench. A weighty darkness.

After a few steps in, he had a change of heart.

Slowly, he took a step backward. And another. And another, and then he backed into the wall.

He turned around and reached for the tunnel entrance, but it had vanished. The entrance had sealed itself off, trapping him inside with ... with something he didn't want to know about.

This darkness was absolute. Vast. Heavy. Darker than dark. It flowed into his lungs with every breath.

His heart pounded so hard he saw red globes floating around him.

He could run screaming further into the tunnel, but that would mean certain death. Besides, he didn't think this was a tunnel at all. A room, maybe. A vestibule.

Perhaps his coffin.

His only option was to throw a card.

Standing perfectly still in the absolute darkness, with a hot, nauseating darkness within that darkness pressing closer to him, he tried slowing his breathing. He stood quietly, letting the evil sniff him, touch him, taste him. It looked into him, saw his fears and magnified them. It saw his shortcomings and embellished them until he saw himself as an insipid cartoon. An uninteresting clown of predictably immoral behavior.

This evil reveled in his sins.

Slowly, very slowly, he reached up to his breast pocket, unbuttoned it and pulled out a card.

"I need a way out of here," he whispered, and bracing for the concussion, threw the card down the tunnel.

The flat concentric circles of blue light flashed only briefly. The darkness muffled, absorbed, the concussion. The darkness, it appeared, was too thick, too substantial, too … *evil* even for the magic.

He hoped to God that the magic hadn't strengthened whatever it was that pressed in on him, so close he could feel it oozing around on his skin.

And yet … and yet he heard the faintest of crackling sounds.

This was similar to the crackling sounds the blue magic made when it melted these tunnels out of the pure rock to begin with.

Was it melting a new tunnel for him?

He didn't want a new tunnel.

All things being equal, he would just as soon go back to the big cavern with the lake and the rocks and the giant coconut and spoiled squash. He had tried to keep track of where he was within the tunnel system, but he had long ago lost his way.

He could live in that big cavern with the lake. He could rest and eat and drink and swim and get himself strong and healthy, and then when ready, he could dive down and find the outlet. If it had an inlet as strong as the river he had ridden on to enter the cavern, then surely it had an outlet. He would find that outlet, swim through it, and be in another moving water system.

He might drown trying, but at least he wouldn't be here, caught in this black web of soul-numbing, paralyzing terror.

Worse, of course, was the nagging feeling that the evil enveloping him was of his own making. It was his own evil, and he needed to accept it.

The crackling noise became louder, as if it was coming closer. But it made no light, so Adam stood still, hands at his sides, eyes wide open, hoping for a glimpse of something that would indicate what the magic had brought him.

Perhaps nothing good. Perhaps nothing at all.

Very slowly, very carefully so as to not make any disturbance, so as to not create any ripples in the clot of evil that had enveloped him, he reached again into his pocket for another card.

He had few cards left. Soon he would be alone down here with no magic to help him.

Should he throw another card? Would adding more magic help? Or would it too, be absorbed, making whatever this was even more powerful and hasten his demise?

"Please, God," he whispered. "Please, God of the underworld. God of my understanding."

He paused for the briefest of moments.

What the hell was the god of his understanding? Did he have any understanding of God at all? *At all?*

"Please. I need my family. I need to get back to my family. They need me."

A deep rumbling arose from beneath his feet. The floor of the tunnel rolled and quaked. Adam took another step backward and put a hand to the tunnel wall to steady himself. The ground buckled, and he sat down before he fell down.

The rumbling stopped, and Adam was left with the distinct impression that it had laughed at him.

The evil had laughed at him.

What was it mocking? His prayer? His need for his family?

The idea that his family needed him?

Perhaps it was right. Perhaps his family didn't need him at all.

He was the one who needed them. He needed their joy, their light, their wonderful, crazy senses of humor. The light they brought to his life.

Why on earth would he have left them to come to Congo to dig wells, when he could have stayed home and helped Lisa find a college, helped Sonja with her homework and her self-esteem, helped Mouse navigate the subtleties of social interaction with her peers?

He was a selfish bastard.

Without a further thought, he flipped the card at the wall, and this time the blue shock wave punched him in the chest and in the flash he saw a door appear, still under crackling blue construction. He heard the sounds as the magic built it out of the plain black rock.

Then the blue flash subsided, and the blackness again closed in, obscuring his view.

Adam slowly and carefully got to his knees. He crawled quietly toward the door, listening as he went. He followed the sound, crawled toward it.

The darkness again pressed close around him, enveloped him, crushed him with its domineering presence.

Hope fled.

He would die here.

He deserved to die here.

He was worthless as a husband, a father, a provider, and come to think of it, he wasn't that great as a hydrologist. His boss was only too happy to give him a lengthy leave of absence.

He had no business acting important, or even competent.

He had an evil in his soul that was so dark and deep and black that he was afraid to let anyone close to him, lest they blow his cover and expose him for the fraud that he was.

Fraud! That was such a nice word for the despicable shit he was.

He should die. This would be a good place to die.

The floor of the tunnel began to move again, only this time it was not laughing at him. Instead, it rocked him with approval.

Adam wanted to die here, and this place would help him.

Abandoning the idea of making it to the door, embracing the end of his life, he curled into a fetal position on the ground. Was there anything he needed to do or think or say before his life ended? He hoped his death would be swift and without suffering.

Without suffering.

But that would not happen at the will of this evil. It would delight in his suffering. His screams would echo through the labyrinth, and the evil would laugh.

The crackling stopped.

Adam barely registered the change, but somewhere in the back of his mind, he knew that the door had been completed.

Could he escape? Was that even possible? Could he die another way that was not at the tormenting hands of this nastiness?

He unwound himself and crawled on his belly toward the door.

He touched it with his fingertips, ran his fingers around the base of it, up along the jamb.

Was there a knob? Was there a lock? Was it just another tantalizing thing that he would never be able to open?

The floor of the tunnel buckled, tossing Adam away from the door.

The evil didn't want him to go.

This wasn't his evil. He didn't need to own this terrible, soul-sucking darkness.

He may have evil in his soul. He may have done appalling things in his life, but he could change. He could do better. He could accept mercy. He could accept grace. He could become a recovered person.

The evil in the tunnel had turned his mind dark. He needed to get to that door, get through that door and slam it behind him. Maybe he could leave this feeling behind and get back to his senses.

He crawled back to the door, but the tunnel floor began to writhe, buckle and twitch, doing its best to keep him from escaping. There was no way he could stand long enough to reach the door handle.

Strange hallucinations of pleasure began to tumble through his mind. He thought of that first swallow of a cold beer after a hot day's work. He remembered the first time he had sex in the back of Mary Jane Moore's father's car. He remembered the look in Chrissie's eyes when she said her vows. He remembered smelling the top of newborn Lisa's head.

He remembered winning a big jackpot at the casino. He remembered the look on that cashier behind her secure little brass gate, her solid, protective cage, as she let a little money out in order to let in a whole lifetime of his desperate gambling addiction.

He recalled the sweetness of that Irish bar maid lifting her skirts to him in the back room of the pub while Chrissie played darts with the pub regulars. The girl was so fresh, so beautiful, her plump cheeks flushed with passion, her chubby thighs delicious, her little squeaks of pleasure egging him on, her long red braid bouncing on the sacks of grain as he took her, feeling like a wild stallion. Oh God, that was so good.

No, it was not good.

Yes, that was great, but it was wrong.

He had been on his honeymoon, for God's sake.

He'd left the girl a big tip, much to Chrissie's disapproval, and he couldn't justify it and he couldn't look his bride in the face.

He saw where this was going. He was being seduced with the promise of more pleasure, but his greatest pleasure would be to get out of there.

He let those memories of extreme pleasure wash over him, but held fast to the fragment of himself that would not succumb. He gritted his teeth against the temptation to just lie back and give up. Let it take him in a state of ecstatic reminiscence.

The evil intertwined the pleasure of his heinous misdeeds with the pleasure of his righteous acts, and that was dangerous.

Adam clung to the concept of right and wrong as he crawled back to the door. He grappled for something to hold on to, to help him stand and reach the knob.

Then something dark and ice cold grabbed his left foot. His tortured foot, swollen and bleeding, had now become whole and good.

Another trick.

He pulled on that foot, and with his other foot, kicked at whatever held it. His kicks landed in open space. Something, and yet nothing had his foot. Something cold, squishy and gelatinous began to suck on it, devouring first his toes, then up his heel, his ankle—

It was so good. It felt wrong, naughty, forbidden, and wonderful. Like he was being swallowed by an orgasm.

He scrambled as hard as he could to get to the door, but the darkness had his foot and was pulling him away from his only means of escape.

He sat up and tried to strike out with his hands, but he touched nothing but dense blackness.

Yet he was being eaten.

Absorbed.

With a burst of energy, he jumped up to his one free foot and lunged at where he thought the doorknob would be.

He landed perfectly, his hand on the lever.

With his last gasp of energy, he pushed the lever down and the door opened.

Adam fell through and with both hands on the door-jamb, pulled his foot through behind him. He grappled for the edge of the door, for the latch, found it, and slammed it behind him.

Instantly, the overpowering dread vanished.

He lay on a cold stone floor, not wanting to move. Wanting only to rest, to sleep, to wake up and discover that this had indeed all been a horrible nightmare.

If that were true, perhaps he would never sleep again.

He didn't know where he was, but wherever it was, it was better than where he had just been. The overwhelming feeling of doom had left him as soon as he shut that door behind him, and he was not about to open it again and succumb to whatever it was that made him want to give up and let it consume him.

Eventually, he sat up and inspected his foot. It was dry and unscathed, except for the ruinous blisters that plagued every attempt at escape from this hell.

And then he realized that he could see those blisters.

Light!

He quickly looked around, startled by the vast dining room he seemed to find himself in. He wanted to explore this new weirdness, but first he had to appreciate the fact that he was safe from that horror, and then he had to take stock of himself now that he could see.

He examined both feet. As blistered, bloody, scabbed and sore as they were, they were intact. He still had a slim deck of cards in his shirt pocket and two giant seeds in his pants pockets. His clothes, while filthy and torn in places, still covered him adequately. The scab on his head had healed as well as could be expected without stitches, the knot almost completely gone.

He needed a shave. And a bath and a meal. Other than that, he was all right. Nothing broken. Nothing damaged beyond repair.

With great effort, he stood and looked around at his surroundings.

He seemed to be in a great stone dining hall, befitting that of a castle.

A fire roared in the massive fireplace at the end of the room, which had been festooned for a great feast.

The table, yards long, had been set with finery, both in decorations with bowls of fruit, but also with fine dinnerware and cutlery. Candles stood white and pristine in their candelabra, waiting to be lit.

Tapestries hung from the high ceiling, the stone floors were covered with thick, intricately-woven rugs. Above him, the high rough-beamed ceiling sported a perfectly aligned array of candled chandeliers, not yet lit.

It was all scaled to Adam's small size.

He touched the giant seeds in his pockets, just to make sure he was still the size of someone who could run through a rat tunnel.

He was.

He wanted nothing more than to go to the fire and warm himself. He wanted to take fruit from the table and eat it. He wanted to investigate this chamber, find a warm bath and then a soft bed and balm for his feet.

He wanted a break.

He needed a day off.

Yet there was something not right about the way the fire flickered in the fireplace. It didn't seem real. It looked more like a photographic loop of a fire, going through the same flame pattern, the same crackle, the same settling log, the same flash of sparks, over and over again.

That wasn't the only thing not quite right about the room. The geometry was off somehow, the proportions growing lengthwise, and then sometimes widthwise, and at times the room itself seemed to flicker as if it were just a mirage, or an image projected onto a screen. It wasn't exactly like the whole Ireland scenario, but it wasn't right.

He didn't trust it.

He didn't trust anything here. He didn't even trust himself.

The door he had entered through—the door that, under normal circumstances, would lead to the evil chamber he had just escaped—had disappeared.

There was nothing here of normal circumstances.

Instead of exploring, he scooted over to a wall, far from where the door used to be, crossed his legs, and waited.

He saw no other doors. This party for what—thirty or forty?—had to come in from somewhere, yet he saw no other means of entrance.

His stomach growled.

The ceiling grew taller, the room a little smaller. A dizzying, swirling moment of vertigo attacked him, then passed.

He was afraid he could look forward to more of that.

After his stomach settled, he looked again with longing at the lavish bowls of fruit on the table.

He put a hand on a seed in his pocket, but it didn't appeal, not when faced with huge bowls of grapes, pears, apples, bananas, plums, kiwi, and more. His mouth watered.

But was it real? And if real, was it safe?

He woofed a sarcastic laugh.

Safe? Really?

"Be bold, Adam," he said out loud. "Don't cower."

He stood on wretchedly painful feet, brushed off his clothes, and while he endeavored to stride to the table, in reality, it was a pathetic old-man limp that got him there.

He put out his hand, and as he reached for the beautifully polished apple, a little electric tingle buzzed his fingers.

He snatched his hand back and regarded the apple. It looked perfectly fine. In fact, it looked red, ripe, juicy, and delicious.

He reached out again, slowly, tentatively, afraid that something could spring from the bowl of fruit and take off his hand.

Nothing happened, and then the tingle again. Like a mild electric shock.

This was some type of a trap. They were expecting him to—

They? What *they?*

"Who are you?" he shouted to the room. "Why are you doing this to me?"

His voice echoed off the massive stone walls as he would expect it to in a normal room. "What's *happening* here?"

He stood in the middle of the room, arms out, palms up, and turned completely around, awaiting an answer.

When he turned back to the table, he was no longer alone.

8

A MAN SAT at the head of the long, formally-set table. He was dressed as a normal man, in a shirt with an open collar, the cuffs rolled up. He seemed to be middle-aged, with plenty of dark brown hair on his head and his forearms, a swarthy complexion, and nice glasses. He didn't look like the king for which this apparent feast had been prepared, nor did he look like any kind of an underworld god that Jolmy imagined.

He looked like a neighbor. A co-worker.

And yet ... he was *here*. In this *place*.

Adam closed his eyes, ran his hands over his face. Again, the idea that this was all just a horrible dream came over him. He rubbed his face hard, and then looked again.

The man smiled at him. He looked relaxed, sitting very casually in the high backed wooden chair that looked vaguely like a throne. "Come," he said. "Sit. I think you deserve a rest."

"I deserve an explanation," Adam said, standing his ground.

Elizabeth Engstrom

"In time," the man said, and picked up an apple. "In the meantime, this one won't hurt you." He held it out.

Adam hesitated. He pointed to the bowl of fruit at the other end of the table.

"I turned off the burglar alarm," the man said and smiled.

Adam was helpless to stop himself from walking straight to the man, to the apple he held out.

The apple seemed normal.

Adam rubbed it on his pant leg while he looked at the man, who sat calmly, comfortably, hands folded in front of him. The man nodded that he should take a bite. "Won't hurt me?"

"Won't hurt you."

Adam bit into it, and sweet, moist deliciousness filled his mouth.

He closed his eyes in ecstasy, his empty stomach roared, and he ate that apple faster than he had ever eaten an apple before in his life.

By the time it was nothing more than a gnawed core, apple juice had run down his chin and onto his hands.

Ravenous hunger consumed him.

"Sit," his host beckoned. He moved the bowl of fruit closer to Adam. "Help yourself."

Adam sat in the proffered chair, took a fine linen napkin from his place setting and wiped his face and hands, then reached for a perfect banana. He peeled and ate that just as quickly. As he reached for a bunch of tantalizing white grapes, he saw that the water glass where he sat was full, beads of condensation sliding down the outside of it.

He picked it up and with a nod from his host, he drank it down with great gasping gulps. Then he reached for the grapes, took them into his hands and sat back in the chair.

Nourishment flowed through his veins. He felt better than he had since … since before he took his girls to the airport. How many days ago was that? Had he been dreaming mere minutes, or had he been lost underground in these tunnels of nonsensical lunacy for days? Weeks?

Months?

The high-backed wooden chair he relaxed into was not all that comfortable, but it was better than sitting on the floor.

He took a deep breath and plucked a grape from the bunch in his hand and popped it into his mouth. Magnificent. Picked at the peak of perfection, as they say on the commercials.

He looked at his host. "Thank you."

The host nodded in response, picked up his wine glass that, Adam now noted, was filled with a dark wine, and tipped it toward Adam in acknowledgement, then he sipped.

"Can you explain—" With a wave of his hand, Adam indicated the entire room with its extravagant party preparations.

"No," the man said. "I don't think it's necessary, nor is it required."

Not the type of response Adam expected from such a seemingly-gracious host. But then, he reminded himself, not everything here is as it appears to be.

"Well then," Adam tried a different tack. "Can I please know who has been so generous with me?"

"That information is irrelevant," the man said. "Suffice it to say that you are a most welcome guest. The others will arrive shortly, and you are welcome to eat and drink your fill."

"The others?"

"You, of course, are the guest of honor."

Adam's hand paused, grape midway to his mouth. "Me?"

"Who else?"

"Why?"

"Why not?"

Why not indeed. Adam looked around. "Might I freshen up?"

His host laughed, a sincere laugh that made him remove his glasses and wipe tears of mirth from his eyes. "Oh," he said. "See there? That's why you are our guest of honor." He cleaned his glasses and placed them back on his nose. He chuckled. "That was a good one."

"How will the other guests get here?" Adam asked— desperate for any information that would give him a clue as to how to get out of here and back to his real life. "I don't see a door."

"Oh, here they are," his host said, "Right on time." In an instant, the room filled with men and women, all dressed in rich clothing that seemed to be from some kind of King's Court of the 1800s. Ladies in silks and satins with their hair piled high and voluminous petticoats, gentlemen wearing tuxedos with waxed moustaches and hair slicked back.

They talked and laughed among themselves as if they had been talking, drinking, and laughing for hours, right here, in what seemed to be an ongoing, perpetual dinner party, but Adam hadn't been able to see them, couldn't hear them.

Until abruptly, he could.

The host rang a little silver bell next to his plate, and the conversation ceased immediately. All eyes turned to Adam.

"We have a guest," the host said simply.

Ladies curtsied, the men bowed, and then they all took their seats at the big table.

This is not real, Adam reminded himself. *This is not real.*

When the food appeared on his plate, thick slices of roasted meat *au jus*, vegetables barely steamed just the way he liked them, freshly baked rolls, dark wine that was full bodied and sweet, but not too sweet, it was hard for him to remember that this was not real.

Conversation went on around him, but it seemed like just so much white noise. He concentrated on eating. He was famished, and every bite was a revelation to his abused body.

No one seemed to be particularly interested in him. Was he just another in a long line of "guests" that came to dinner?

More important, to what end was he the guest?

As soon as he finished his meal, it vanished, and a dessert pudding of some sort appeared.

He looked down the row of plates. The same pudding was on every plate, and people began dipping their spoons, exclaiming over its creamy deliciousness, and drinking dessert wine from tiny wine glasses.

This is not real. None of this is real.

He wasn't going to get any answers by sitting here filling his belly.

He drank another glass of water, which had magically refilled, wiped his lips, pushed back his chair, and stood up.

The room quieted. He had everyone's attention.

He held up his port wine glass. "To our host," he said.

At first, the guests looked at each other in confusion. Then one man stood and held up his wine glass in salute. "To our host," he said. Others followed, until they all stood, and the woman sitting next to Adam raised her glass and said, "To Oliver."

The name hit Adam like a cannonball in his gut.

Oliver!

The others gasped and stared at her in astonishment.

She hung her head in shame, and an instant later, she vanished. A moment after that, her pudding, all the dishes and cutlery, wine and water glasses at her place also disappeared.

Oliver, no longer smiling, acknowledged the accolades of the assembled guests with raised glass and then a sip. Everyone seemed happy to retake their seats and resume their conversations.

Adam collapsed back into his chair and looked long and hard at his host.

Oliver.

He looked very familiar. Too familiar. Maddeningly familiar.

Adam's blood pressure rose. His face heated. He wanted nothing more than to leap over the table and punch that smug motherfucker in the teeth.

Settle down, he counseled himself. *The point is to get out of here.*

"Sorry about Lady Dulcinea," Oliver said, indicating the empty chair next to Adam. "She means well, but sometimes exercises poor judgment."

"To where has she been banished?" Adam asked.

"My dear man," Oliver said, "she was here as a guest of the wheel of fortune, but she was on shaky ground from the outset. As you can see, she broke her wheel with her lack of judgment."

"And am I subject to this same wheel?"

"No," Oliver said, smiling. "Of course not. You have your own." He sipped his wine. "But I must say, it is beginning to look downright rickety."

"I don't understand the rules," Adam said.

"None of us do," Oliver replied.

"How is that fair?"

Again, Oliver laughed, this time so robustly that he stopped conversation at the table. "Our *guest*"—he emphasized the word *guest*—"thinks that life is not fair."

The others at the table began to laugh as well, a little too hard, a little too long, showing way too many teeth.

The more Adam looked at them, the more they began to look like caricatures.

But there was no question that his belly was full of food, and there was the flavor of wine on his tongue. So how much of this was real, and how could he escape it and get out?

He wanted to get out. He wanted to go home.

Now. He wanted to go now.

He stood again, and one by one, the guests quieted. All faces turned to him expectantly, smiling, as if he was about to entertain them further.

Slowly, he unbuttoned his shirt pocket, removed a card, and then buttoned the pocket again.

He had drawn the King of Swords.

Surely the King of Swords outranked Oliver, king of scumbags.

He held up the card and showed it first to Oliver, who raised an eyebrow. Then he showed it to everyone else at the table.

A few women gasped.

Adam looked at Oliver. "Do you know what this means?"

"I have an idea."

"Will this destroy you, and them, and this whole—this whole room?"

"Destroy? No." Oliver leaned forward. "But it does not show the gratitude I would expect from one who has so liberally availed himself of my hospitality."

Adam had enough of Oliver's overt smugness. "Thank you for dinner," Adam said. He bowed, plucked a banana from the fruit bowl, then turned and flicked the card at the wall.

The blue horizontal circles blasted out, knocking Adam back against the table, and then when the table disappeared from behind him, landed him on his butt on the ground.

In a tunnel.

In a dirt tunnel, with the little blue flame burning on the ground next to him. The dining table, Oliver, and all the weird guests had vanished.

Had they ever been there? Had he fallen asleep here in this tunnel and dreamed it all? Had it been another dream within a dream?

The banana was still in his hand.

He shoved it into a cargo pocket in his pants, picked up the blue flame with his fingers and closed his eyes in gratitude. He hadn't died, at least not yet—at least he didn't think he had.

Wait.

Had he died?

Had he died at the hands of the rebel thug in the jungle? Was this hell? Was this his purgatory?

That was too much for him to think about. If he was indeed dead, then he had all of eternity to muse those mysteries.

For the moment, he had what he assumed was food in his belly, magic in his pocket, and fruit for later. He was back in a black tunnel, but somehow that and the little blue flame next to him was more comforting than he expected. He almost sobbed with tremendous relief for what oddly enough, had begun to seem like normalcy.

Oliver and his weird guests could have turned out to be almost anything.

They could have been vampires, even, enriching his blood with that high fat dinner for their after-dinner snack.

And what was he to make of Oliver? What was *he*, of all people, doing here in this place, in Adam's nightmare, in his own personal and private hell?

Oliver had been part of his personal, private hell for years.

The little blue flame wasn't going to last for long, and he really should use it to great advantage while he had it, exploring the tunnel, searching for a way out.

Perhaps endlessly searching for a way out.

He couldn't make himself move. Exhaustion overtook him, and with his companion flame in the palm of his hand, he tipped over onto his side and slept where he lay.

He dreamed of Sonja. His middle daughter, the one who somehow got lost amidst the academic genius of his older daughter and the mischievous baby Mouse. She was the homemaker. She wanted to cook, to sew, to knit. She wanted to excel in home economics and reading high school romance novels, and cared nothing for school or science or cell phones, Twitter, Facebook, or email. She was invisible in the family, ignored—not on purpose or by design—by Adam and Chrissie, only because she took up so little space. Her needs were few, her two sisters demanding all of their parents' time and attention.

Little Sonja had been left to herself, and she was doing just fine.

Right? She was doing just fine, right?

In his dream, fair little Sonja, wearing a real bra for the first time, at least the first time he had noticed, was carrying a beautifully, expertly made chocolate cake on a crystal, footed cake plate. She moved quietly from room to room with the perfectly-iced cake, waiting for someone to compliment her, showing it to everybody, but nobody took the time to comment on her masterpiece. This was a cake that could take a blue ribbon at the county fair, but nobody in the family noticed.

Adam watched her as if watching a newsreel. He saw himself reading on the couch with Lisa as Sonja paraded her cake through the living room, completely ignored. She walked through the home office, where Chrissie was concentrating on the family bookkeeping chores. She walked out the back door, past Mouse, who was dressed in an old fairy Halloween costume, digging a trench for no particular reason in the back yard.

Sonja walked out the back gate, and handed it to a boy, who waited in the alley behind their house.

"I made you a cake," she told him, and he licked chocolate from her fingers as they gazed into each others' eyes.

No, Sonja! Adam squirmed in his sleep.

He watched as the boy led her by the hand to the back seat of an old car, parked in the alley. They ate the cake and then kissed.

Adam's stomach churned as the boy unzipped Sonja's jeans and pulled them down, kissing her thighs, her knees, then pulled them off.

Her little pink flowered panties quickly followed, as Sonja worked on the boy's belt.

Clearly, they had done this before.

The boy, older, in his twenties, used no protection as Sonja climbed into his lap. By the time they were finished, they both had chocolate icing all over their faces and hands.

"I love you," Sonja said.

"I love you, too," the boy said, "I will love you forever, but I have to go now."

"Take my love with you," Sonja said, and handed him a handful of cake, which he loaded into the cargo pocket of his pants.

The boy set Sonja down on the seat, zipped his pants, and got out of the car. Sonja turned to face Adam in his dream. "Hi, Dad. I'm going to have a baby. My baby will love me, because it has to. It will love me with unconditional love. You don't love me, because you don't have to. I kind of like you, but I will love my baby more."

"No, no, honey, that's not right. Please don't do that to yourself, you have no idea—"

Adam woke up, sweating, with a sob in his chest.

He picked up the little blue flame and its companionship comforted him, as he realized that he had indeed ignored his middle daughter. He didn't know whether or not she was having sex, but he should know. How could he be so blind, so stupid as to let her engage in activities he knew nothing about? His job was to protect her and he'd done a piss poor job of it.

The sob broke through. "Sonja, I'm so sorry," he said.

He remembered her working in the kitchen with Jolmy's wife and daughters, learning her homemaking skills.

That's what she wanted. She wanted to be a wife and a mother. She had no other ambitions. She didn't want to go to school to learn a trade. She wanted to be a mother, and that was a project she could get started on right away.

Now it all made sense. Just as he had gone to school to learn hydrology and the finer points of what he would end up doing for a living, Sonja was learning to cook and bake and be a mother, as that was her one and only ambition in life.

He also remembered seeing her play games, sometimes rough and tumble games, with the village boys. She was learning the art of flirtation.

Had she been having sex with one or more boys in the village?

Lisa had been busy teaching; Adam had been busy installing waterline; Chrissie had been busy helping the village women get their little business going; Mouse was busy climbing trees and chasing down all the wildlife she could find.

Who paid attention to Sonja?

She was *twelve* for God's sake!

But maybe it was all a dream. Maybe, like that weird dinner event, this was just a dream within a dream. Maybe it wasn't true at all. Maybe Sonja was still innocent, maybe …

But even as he thought that, he knew the truth. He knew the signs. He knew that boys came around. He knew that she dressed provocatively at times, padding her little bra. He saw her rub up against some of the village boys, and he said nothing. He said nothing and he did nothing. He didn't want to deal with it. Wasn't that Chrissie's job?

No, of course not. It was his job as Sonja's father. Keep her safe. Protect her.

He had failed.

He hadn't wanted Sonja. He only wanted Lisa, his firstborn. He wanted to be with her every waking minute, to help her eat, to help her walk. He taught Lisa her alphabet, and her colors, and numbers, and then he taught her to read. He took her out on jobs with him when she was old enough, and engaged her curiosity.

He loved Lisa, he lived for Lisa.

Sonja had been a distraction.

Lisa was Adam's. Sonja belonged to Chrissie.

Sick about the truth of himself, Adam jumped to his feet, grabbed the blue flame, put it on his shoulder and with a renewed resolve to get out of this fucking hellhole, started walking.

It didn't seem to matter which way he went, it all led to weirdness. His rickety wheel of fortune, as Oliver had said.

Oliver. Adam spit. Fucking Oliver.

Adam's failing here was that he wasn't taking advantage of the weirdness. If only he could figure out the clues in each strange situation, he could break the magic and return above ground. Return to the village. Catch the next plane to Minneapolis.

He had to be smarter. He had to use the magic with a little wisdom, instead of haphazardly.

Oliver had said that Lady Dulcinea had broken her wheel of fortune by using bad judgment.

With his past coming into very close and disturbing focus, Adam was clearly the king of bad judgment.

Was it too late to change that?

He didn't really know how. How could he know that throwing that card would vaporize Oliver and the whole room and give him the blue flame again, all at once? He could never have predicted that.

His stash of magic cards was dwindling.

His wheel of fortune was looking mighty rickety, indeed.

Still, he walked. He strode with purpose to only God knew where, on miserable feet, a fresh dose of sorry desperation in his heart.

9

THE DIRT TUNNEL continued endlessly. It twisted right, and then left, it dipped down, it doubled back on itself, it rose upward. It continually divided, giving Adam myriad choices of which tunnel to take, and he just took the closest one, not caring, not thinking, just moving forward on tortured feet.

Nothing assaulted him. He found no crazy rooms, no mysterious doors, and he needed no magic. He just walked on feet that were raw, it seemed, to their very bones.

And on he walked.

He ate the banana, and the giant pumpkin seed.

Little flickers of movement continued out of the corner of his eyes, but he no longer startled at them. His heart no longer pounded with the thought of someone else being in the tunnel with him, real or imagined. He no longer cared. He had no energy to spare. He was beyond exhausted, and his feet were so beyond repair that he didn't even feel them anymore. The skull-cracking pain in his head returned with every beat of his laboring heart, with every agonizing step.

He just walked.

His tongue swelled, his lips cracked with thirst. Occasionally, he sucked moisture that trickled from the dirt wall, but it just resulted in a mouthful of gritty mud. Now and then he pulled a root from the roof or wall of the tunnel and chewed it for moisture and for something to taste. They, too, tasted like dirt.

He preferred the dirt tunnel to the black glass tunnel that led to Oliver and his crazy dinner party. This dirt tunnel seemed real. When he was in the dirt tunnel, he had the tiniest twinge of hope that some time, some day, he would exit this misery and be back up above ground.

On he marched, for days, it seemed, miles upon miles, until his steps grew unsteady, his leg muscles cramped, and still he managed to put one foot in front of the other until he stumbled and fell, face first, onto the ground.

The little blue flame winked out.

He lay still, too exhausted to move.

This is it. I shall die here. Chrissie, Lisa, Sonja, Mouse, I love you all. I love you and I failed you. Forgive me.

Adam slowly pulled into a fetal position, closed his eyes and waited to die.

Memories flooded over him, and he let them come.

This is what happens when you die.

Your life flashes before you.

He remembered meeting Chrissie, their whirlwind romance, their wedding in her parents' living room, small, intimate, to save money for their extravagant honeymoon in Ireland.

He failed to keep the vows he made that day, the first of which was fidelity, and that didn't take long.

The miracle of Lisa, growing in Chrissie's tummy. Chrissie would put Adam's hands on her belly when they were in bed together, and he would talk, sing, tell jokes to the little thing growing inside. It was so magical.

Even so, while at a conference, he got a twenty dollar blow job from a hooker in the hotel elevator while his pregnant wife slept upstairs.

And when Lisa was born, he could not believe his good fortune. A perfect baby, a perfect wife, a good job, a nice, modest apartment, a small car, they lived within their means.

He had amassed tremendous secret debt. Chrissie would find out about it when he died.

Chrissie had wanted another baby right away, and Adam did not. He wanted to spend time with the baby they had. They argued. "In time," he said, over and over again.

In time, he said. (*When he paid off his gambling debts.*) They would have another baby in time, let's enjoy Lisa while she's little.

"It's time now," she said, more than once. "I want the kids to be close, to have a relationship. My brother is six years older than I am. We were never close."

"We have time," Adam said, more than once. "Let's get a little more financially secure, first."

Chrissie punished him. She would not accept finances as his reason, and he couldn't tell her the real reason. So she darkened their utopia. Shadows came between them, cold rain fell on their meals together, on their family outings. Even Lisa, after she learned to walk, would walk one to the other and take their hands and try to get them to sit together, to sit next to each other, but they did not. Would not.

And then one night, sick of the cold shoulder, Adam gave in.

He reached for her in the night, and she was only too eager to accommodate his desire, then, and every opportunity thereafter until she conceived. It wasn't love making, it was baby creating, and these acts of biology without closeness left Adam lonelier than ever. He spent all his time with Lisa, while Chrissie prepared for the new baby, a girl. Sonja.

He gambled more, and fell deeper into debt.

Their parents were delighted with the new granddaughter, of course, and set up college funds for both girls, but all Adam saw when he looked at Sonja was money flying out the window. More music lessons. More dance lessons. More clothes. More expensive weekends away. More babysitters.

He saw only his failures as a husband, a father, a provider.

He paid his gambling debt with their college funds and then tried, desperately, terribly desperately, horribly desperately, to refill those funds. But the craps table, the blackjack table, the poker table, the smug cashier on the other side of that little brass cage took it all. Took all the girls' money! Took it all and then more and more upon more. He could barely live with the horrific secret. He wanted to fix it before he had to confess. And now, Chrissie would find out.

He had only cared about himself.

That's why he went to Congo. To get away. Away from the family, away from the casinos. Away from his sins, away from his indiscretions, away from his responsibilities. He needed to get away from it all.

He needed to get away from himself.

And now here he was, dying, with only the company of himself. His own wretched self.

He'd done other things, too. When Lisa got a ferret as a gift, he took it to the woods and let it go, telling her that it had escaped its cage and got away. He watched her cry for days with a hard heart, but he'd be damned if he'd have a weasel in his house. Lisa tearfully begged for another, and even Chrissie joined in, but Adam flatly refused.

Ditto Sonja's ant farm that she got for Christmas from his parents. No insects in his house on purpose for God's sake. Why would anybody bring ants into the house on purpose? Ridiculous. He just threw it out and disavowed knowledge of its fate. Chrissie, Lisa, and Sonja turned the house upside down looking for it, and he had stood by with what he hoped was an innocent look on his face, shrugging at the mysterious disappearance.

Eventually, Sonja decided one of her little girlfriends had stolen it, and despite Adam's earnest counsel against shunning the accused, the little girls' sweet, innocent, Barbie doll friendship ended in heartbreak for both of them.

Such small things he'd done caused such unnecessary grief to those he loved.

And then Mouse.

Oh God, Mouse …

Grief, sadness, and regret gripped a handful of his gut and squeezed. The pain curled him up into a ball of pain and misery, and he began to sob.

Oh God, Mouse.

❧

"Is it alive?"

"Shhh. Yes, it's alive, but it's old and sick and very, very sad."

"What is it?"

"I'm not sure."

Adam didn't know he'd been asleep until he was awakened by whispers, and something sliding around on his legs. He lay very still, listening. Maybe it would be best if they thought he was dead. Or still sleeping. Certainly they could see he was not a threat to them.

"Will it hurt us?"

"I don't think so."

"Do we kill it?"

"No, it is dying on its own."

Startled, Adam drew his legs up to his chest and wrapped his arms around his knees. "Hello?" His voice sounded weak and scratchy.

"It speaks!"

"Yes." He cleared his throat. "Who's there?" he asked.

"We are here," one soft, faintly female voice replied in the darkness, and again, something slithered around him.

"Are you snakes?"

"Are you snakes?" the voice repeated.

There was much discussion among them in hushed whispers. Then: "What are snakes?"

One of them slithered past Adam's head. He reached out and pushed it away. It felt like a snake. He shivered with the thought that he was sleeping in a nest of snakes. Talking snakes. Oh, God. Was *this* real? "What are you then?"

"We are people," the voice said. "We live here. What are you?"

"I am a human, and I don't live here," Adam said. Hope rose. If they lived here, perhaps they would know how to help him get back to the surface. "I live above the ground. In the sunlight. I came here by accident and don't know how to get back."

He sensed the snake things retreat from him, their dry slithering a raspy, strange, musical sound. Again, they whispered softly to one another.

Adam sat up and scooted to the side of the tunnel, resting his back against it. If they were going to attack him, best to have his back against the wall.

He heard rustling and then the one spoke again, closer to him than he realized.

He flinched, it was so close to his ear.

"Are you God?" the snake asked.

Adam considered this. Could he be a god to these people? Would they help him if he said he was?

Could he manipulate these simple people by claiming to be their god?

Stop it. Stop manipulating people! Have you learned nothing down here?

But he would do anything …

But then how could a god need the help of those he supposedly created?

As tempting as it might be to call himself a god to a race of sentient snakes, it wasn't true and to do it wasn't right.

"No," he said. "I am lost."

"Are you dying?"

"Yes," Adam said. "If I can't get back above ground into the sunlight, I will die."

The snake thing retreated and the whispering again commenced.

Adam began to cough, a harsh, rasping, lung-ripping cough that hurt his ribs and scorched his throat. His dehydrated lower lip split down the middle and the tang of blood flooded his mouth.

"I need water," he gasped.

Again the slithering, but this time, when the snake thing spoke, Adam was prepared for it to be close. Still, closer than he expected.

"We can take you to water," she—*it*—said.

"Please," Adam choked out.

"But Oliver said—"

"*Oliver?*" Adam fell again to coughing. As soon as he regained his breath, he responded. "FUCK OLIVER!"

When he heard himself say that, he remembered the last time he said those words with that wrath.

It was all he could do to keep from thumping that smug fuck at his fancy dinner table with all those weird people. But assault hadn't seemed to be the answer to his situation, so he had restrained himself.

But here he was again. *Oliver.* Oliver had something to do with his being here. Oliver had his smelly little fingers in every aspect of Adam's life, even here! It seemed like there was nothing Adam could do to rid himself of goddamned Oliver.

What else did he have to sacrifice to that sorry bastard?

Desperately sorry for his antagonizing outburst to these snake things, these "people," he calmed himself and again addressed those weird creatures who could take him to the life-saving water. "Please," he said. "I'm so sorry. Can you take me to the water? Can you save my life?"

"Oliver said you would be worth saving, if you yourself believed that to be true," the snake said.

"Is Oliver your god?" Adam asked.

"No, Oliver lives here. He is people, like us."

"He is not like me?"

"No, he is people, like us."

Adam tried to remember Oliver sitting at the head of that ostentatious table. Had he been a snake thing? He was certainly a snake, but was he an actual serpent, like these people? Did he have legs? Feet?

Did he have a tail? Did he slither when he moved?

As dream memories go, he could not quite remember if Oliver was a serpent with a head, arms, and hands sitting in that chair. Did his tail curl under the table?

What about the others at that weird dinner party? Were there serpent bodies beneath those fancy clothes? Did Oliver's tail wind around the tails of others at the table? Were they communicating in that way while he innocently ate their food and tried to take them at their word?

Could have been.

In the ways of dreams, Adam could barely remember Oliver's face. Only that he knew it, he knew that face as well as he knew his own.

Fucking Oliver.

Spent, Adam let his head hang and let the hot ball of emotion rise through his chest to the back of his throat. He was out of food, out of strength, out of energy, out of hope. "I don't know if I am worth saving," he said softly. "I am a wreck." He pulled the remaining shirt sleeve from his waistband—the other having been lost long ago— wiped his face and blew his nose. "But if you help me, I will work to be worthy of your trust." He sucked in a ragged breath. "Oliver has no right to judge me."

Oliver. That shit. That marriage-wrecking piece of worthlessness. *He* was the one who held the keys to Adam's fate? Oh, that's good. That's rich.

"You tell Oliver ..." Adam paused. He did not want to alienate these creatures who could help him. If ever there was a time to be truthful, to be real, to be whole, to be honest and not manipulative, this was it.

What was the truth? Fuck Oliver? That was the truth. But that wasn't going to get him out of here. He sighed in resignation. "Tell Oliver I will be grateful," he said.

"Oliver wants your magic," the voice said.

Of course he does. He wants everything.

Adam patted his shirt pocket that held the few remaining cards. "I will give you half," he said. "And when I get out, I will leave behind what I have not used."

Again, the serpents conferred.

"We will lead you to water, but you must carry us."

Their slithering sounds made a certain chorus as the whole pack of them approached him. He had doubts about his ability to carry himself, much less heavy-bodied creatures.

Slowly, painfully, Adam got to his feet and stood stoically, gritting his teeth as serpents nosed around his screaming, swollen feet, ankles, and then began to wind their way up his legs. There seemed to be many of them, wrapping around his waist, winding up his torso to his arms, around his neck. He gritted his teeth against his compulsion to slap them off, to run screaming into the darkness, but after a few moments, they settled.

They were very heavy.

Adam began walking. His feet were so swollen they seemed like hot baked potatoes on the ends of his legs.

Still, he limped along, bent over, carrying what seemed to be tons of thick, living ropes draped around him, tightening, loosening, sliding, moving relentlessly around him.

Unnerving didn't begin to describe it.

He was tired. Exhausted. Dehydrated.

One of the snakes whispered directions in his ear, but he was certain he was no closer to water than he had been when they started out.

He began to stumble, and when he did, the snakes shifted, writhing around him.

"Are we nearly there?" he asked.

"Nearly there?" was the reply. "Are we nearly there?"

Were they asking him? Why would they ask him? They were the ones giving directions. "Please," he said. "My feet ... I am so tired ... I don't think I can ..."

Just as he thought he could not bear another step, he heard it.

Water.

Thundering water—a waterfall—echoing in a giant chamber.

Had they come upon it suddenly, or had he been so caught up in his own misery he failed to hear it?

How could he fail to hear this?

Maybe Oliver—that fuck—took him to his absolute breaking point every time.

Had Oliver orchestrated all of this? Had Oliver ordered his kidnapping, given him the magic cards, made him walk through endless tunnels for miles, for days, skirting death at every turn?

No, of course not. Oliver was not in Congo. He was back in Minneapolis.

Chrissie was back in Minneapolis, too. He had left her alone there for three months while he came to Congo to escape responsibilities. To escape himself, he had left his wife at home in close proximity, very close proximity, to Oliver.

He couldn't blame Oliver for this. Truth be told, he couldn't really blame Oliver for anything.

Not even Mouse.

Adam shook off his supreme annoyance at himself and leaned forward, hoping the weight of the snakes would help propel him toward the water.

Water!

Adrenaline shot through him and gave him energy to make final steps.

"Turn left," the voice said.

He obeyed, and cool water sprayed across his face.

One by one, in some apparent order, the snakes descended sliding their loops down and off him. They rustled gently, pooled at his feet.

Adam reveled in the feeling of mist wetting his shirt, his pants. He let it run in rivulets down his face. He opened his mouth, and though he couldn't catch enough to swallow, it soothed his parched lips and tongue.

He wanted to laugh, to shout out that he was still alive into the misty cavern but first, he had business to conduct.

In the total darkness, Adam couldn't see the creatures that had brought him here, couldn't see the gigantic cavern he sensed in front of him, couldn't see the waterfall, but he could hear it.

Water was life. Water meant safety, water was transportation, and water inexorably flowed to lakes, rivers, oceans. If he could get into the water, he could be saved. He *would* be saved.

He closed his eyes and held his arms out to embrace the icy spray that wet him.

"Thank you," he whispered in gratitude.

"You owe us the magic," the serpent said.

As before, when Adam considered telling them he was their god, he now considered reneging on the deal to give up half of his precious magical cards.

He paused, thinking about it.

He didn't really know what lay ahead of him, but he knew this was the end of his association with the serpents. What could they do if he failed to keep his part of the bargain? Besides, it was Oliver who wanted the magic. They were doing his bidding. What did he owe Oliver?

Nothing. Not a goddamned thing.

And yet ... they had kept their part of the bargain. This was their realm, their home. They knew this place, and he did not. It could be that they could do him real damage if he skated from his obligation.

And yet ... the magic. It was only by the grace of the magic he was able to stay alive this long in this hellish place. What if he needed it?

If he needed it and he didn't have it, he would die.

Did Oliver care about that?

No. Oliver didn't give a shit.

Maybe he would just give up a few cards. They didn't need to know how many he had.

He sat down on the damp ground. The serpents assembled around him, crawling around his feet, his legs, over his lap, restlessly moving as if they could read his mind and knew of his hesitation to keep his part of the bargain.

What was he thinking? They could see. Of course they could see in this darkness. They could see how many cards he had left. They could see that he was more of a snake than they were, his temptations to cheat them were the temptations he had to cheat everybody, all the time.

The serpents closed in.

Was this an aggressive move?

Adam recoiled, but they had him surrounded. There was no escape, except to jump into the waterfall that was so close the spray wet his clothes.

The snake things were more eager to get the magic to take to Oliver than they were to wrestle him for it.

They could probably do great damage to him if he tried to cheat them. At minimum, they would get some of the magic, and perhaps they knew how to use it better than he did. At worst, he could lose all the magic and be stuck here with nothing.

Surely Oliver knew how to use the magic. He was an asshole. A snake. The king of all snakes.

And by even considering cheating on the deal, he saw himself as the snake he was, too. In comparison, actually, Oliver was not so bad.

Adam unbuttoned his shirt pocket and removed the remaining cards. He counted out eight then put four back in his pocket.

He blindly held out the other four, and a soft hand gently took them from him. Small fingers grazed his own.

A hand! With fingers! What *were* these creatures, anyway? What did they look like in the light?

Once they had the cards, the snakes retreated. Adam had a moment of panic at the thought of being left alone again. They were not such great company, but at least they were company.

He needed to see the water, the waterfall, the whole situation, so he would know how to proceed. They got him to water, but he still had to get back to the surface of the earth. Back to the village. Back to his family in Minnesota so he could make his confession and then make his amends.

He so desperately needed to make his amends.

He took one of his four remaining cards and flicked it into the cavern.

The concussion was lost in the enormous grotto, but the flash of blue concentric circles illuminated what lay ahead just long enough for him to see that he was sitting on a rock outcropping. A very thin ledge.

To the left of him, a stunning waterfall fell from enormous height, and fell hundreds more feet below him. There was nothing but emptiness to the right. Behind him, the dark black, endless tunnel.

They had taken him to water, but he had no access to it, except to jump to his death.

Tricked. Again. Tricked.

Fucking Oliver.

As his eyes again grew accustomed to the dark of the cavern and tunnel, he saw that even though the magic card had not given him access to the body of water way below, it had again gifted him with the slight blue flame. It burned on the ground right next to him.

He was grateful for the flame, the one almost-constant in this ridiculously long and twisting underground ordeal. And now the two of them were together again for the end.

Adam and his blue flame. Together forever.

He picked it up between his thumb and forefinger and held it above the serpents who were slithering back into the tunnel.

"Hey!" he called after them. "What now?"

One of them turned back to look at him. In the pale blue light, Adam recognized her face. She had sat across from him at Oliver's dinner party.

"Hey," the serpent replied, then glided into the darkness. "What now?"

Yes, yes, now he was certain he had lost his mind.

Adam inched closer to the edge of the precipice. He held the light out over the abyss, but its light was swallowed up by the mammoth cavern.

Adam got to his knees, and braced with one hand on the wall of the tunnel, got to his horrifically painful feet. They were so raw and swollen he thought they might burst with the pressure of his weight.

He held the little blue flame up, but it illuminated only his immediate surroundings. He saw nothing but the ledge he stood on and the walls of the tunnel. Ahead of him was the great unknown.

As he stood facing the enormous cavern, the thundering water to his left, the pool, or river, or whatever, way below him, he contemplated his miniscule importance in the world, both above and below ground.

He was inconsequential to everyone but himself. This waterfall didn't care. Those snake things didn't care. The tunnels didn't care. The magic didn't care.

And Chrissie didn't care.

When he had put the four of them on the plane to Minneapolis, he knew that was the end of their marriage. He just hadn't wanted to face it until now, until just this minute. He hadn't had the courage to face it until just now, *right now*, as he faced death and was about to meet his maker. Having his girls come to Congo was a last-ditch effort to save his family, and he had failed.

Failure.

He had lost them. All of them, by being a prick.

And now, here he stood on the precipice. Again.

Clearly, he had two choices: go back into the tunnel, or go forward, dropping most assuredly to his death hundreds of feet below. Chances are, he'd be smashed to pieces on rocks before ever hitting the water and drowning in the freezing, crushing, churning, maelstrom.

There was no choice, not really. He couldn't go back.

His chances of surviving in the water were perhaps one in a million, but he had no chance at all if he returned to the tunnel. In the tunnel he would starve, die of infected feet, die of thirst.

He wanted to sit and wait, to torture himself further by reviewing his life, to make promises to God, to pray, to try to make himself right with his life, to make himself right with his death.

But that was just postponing the inevitable.

"God save me," he whispered, cupped the blue flame close to his chest, and leaped off the ledge.

10

ONCE AIRBORNE, survival instincts took over. Unexpectedly desperate to live, Adam windmilled his arms to try to stay upright, to keep his balance as he fell through the darkness. He wanted to land in the water as vertical as possible. He crossed his legs at the ankles, hoping to slice through the water like a needle with little drag. That would be his best chance of surviving. Falling from this height and landing on his back or his belly would be the end of him.

Of course if he landed on rocks, all this would have been an exercise in futility. Perhaps it was, anyway.

The blue flame stuck to the front of his shirt.

He fell for a long time, longer than he imagined he could ever fall. Time slowed, warped here the way geometry and proportions of the dining room had bent, the way the tunnels had elongated. In slow motion, he fell until he thought perhaps this was another aspect of the nightmare: the falling dream. He would fall forever. Surely he would awaken in Jolmy's house to the sounds of the family rising and getting ready for their day.

Please God, let it be so.

Then he sensed the water coming up beneath him. The splash of the waterfall as it poured into the pool came back into focus. He anticipated the coolness of the water, the increased spray as it soaked him.

Time may have slowed, but his heart raced. He squinted his eyes and waited to either smash on a rock and wake up in—*what, heaven*?—or sink deeply into what he hoped was normal water and not something underworld-weird that would keep him submerged until he drowned.

He crossed his arms over his chest, took a deep breath, and braced himself for impact.

He knifed through the water almost as he expected, except that no water washed up his nose, nothing cold surrounded him.

The little blue flame on his chest did not extinguish. Instead, it had created a bubble around itself and, there-fore, him.

He could breathe!

Adam hit the water perfectly vertical, and then the current swept him in great, dizzying black circles. Without the protection of the blue air bubble he would certainly have drowned. As it was, his heart pounded loudly in his ears, and he had a hard time catching his breath. Breathing normally was out of the question. All around him was black water. He could only see down the length of his body and the shiny interior of the weird bubble in the blue light.

The swirling eddy eventually spit him out and he shot into the current, going quickly in some dark direction. All he could see was the blue flame, still sitting on his chest, illuminating the strange envelope of air. He must glow in the darkness of this cavern, this lake, this river.

Do you see me, Oliver? Are you watching?

The river sped him along at a startling speed, up and over rocks, around eddies and over small falls. He was small, and the magic insulated him. He tried to remain flexible, to just go with the flow and let the bubble do its job. As long as the blue light held, he had hope of survival.

He wasn't dead yet.

But the blue light was not going to last forever, and when it went out, he would be on his own.

At one point the river slowed, and for a moment, Adam was certain he saw stars in the night sky. He cried out to them, as if talking to a taxi driver. "Stop! Stop here!" but there was no driver, and there was no stopping. Immediately, he was whipped around again, over another waterfall, and back into darkness. Gingerly, he touched the inside of the bubble. It seemed firm. Tough.

I will survive!

All he could think about was getting home to his wife and daughters. He would beg their forgiveness. He would do anything, *anything*, to be welcomed back into their love, into their home, into his wife's affections.

He needed to make it right with Sonja.

And with Mouse.

Oh God, Mouse.

New Year's Eve, eleven years ago.

Adam had planned to go to an office New Year's Eve party, and take 4-year-old Lisa with him. Chrissie objected. She didn't want to be left alone with Sonja, still a toddler, on New Year's Eve. They'd been fighting about it for a week. Chrissie wanted to dress up and go to a local hotel ballroom, drink champagne, dance the night away, kiss at midnight. She had been feeling like nothing but a dingy mommy, with old elastic-sprung underwear who smelled always of sour milk and baby poop. She needed to dress up and feel like a woman again. She wanted to speak adult language with new, interesting adults.

Adam didn't care what Chrissie wanted.

He took his daughter and went to his office party. He hadn't even invited Chrissie. Getting a babysitter on New Year's Eve was impossible, and taking a toddler with them was out of the question.

He was convinced that Lisa needed to be introduced to society life from an early age so she would grow up confident and able to navigate all social situations. It was a mistake, of course; nobody brought children to an adult party where booze flowed freely. All his coworkers were dressed to the nines, drinking champagne and flirting shamelessly with one another. The entire staff was in party attire except him, who showed up in standard work clothes, shirt and khakis, and his daughter in little flowered lavender Oshkosh overalls.

Lisa was only four, and not suited for such an event. She was bored, got cranky, and eventually fell asleep on the couch in his boss's office.

Adam drank too much, took one of the secretaries out into the hall, pushed her up against the wall, kissed her long and deep, and ground his erection against her thigh. Then he tried the same trick with a couple of other secretaries, with varying degrees of success. He drank more then drove home, flirting with a DUI—or worse— with his little girl in the car.

When he got home, he found a neighborhood girl dozing on the sofa, and Sonja sleeping soundly in her crib.

No Chrissie.

He paid the babysitter, put Lisa to bed, and waited.

In the morning, a hungry Lisa, dragging her blankie, woke him up. Apparently, he had pulled a throw over himself and gone to sleep on the couch. Sonja was in her crib crying. She needed a fresh diaper and a bottle. Lisa wanted breakfast.

No Chrissie.

Adam downed a beer to quell his raging hangover.

When his wife finally came home about noon, she was wearing a slinky, sexy, silver party dress Adam had never seen before.

"Where the hell have you been?"

She met his fury unblinking, standing eye to eye with absolute self-righteousness. "Out."

"All night? Out all night? What about our kids?" Adam tried very hard not to yell.

To Chrissie's credit, she kept her voice calm. "What about them? They're all right, aren't they?"

"They are, no thanks to you."

She swept past him and he grabbed her arm, harder and tighter than he expected, but his headache was in charge of his anger, and his anger was in charge of his strength.

"Ouch!" She whirled and slapped him.

He released her immediately. He hadn't meant to grab her so hard, he just wanted to talk to her, to find out where she had been, what she had been doing.

She fixed him with an unapologetic expression he had never before seen on her face. It was a challenge. Her eyes said, "You fuck with me one more time and I'm outta here."

He believed her threat. And he'd had no right to grab her the way he did.

But she had been the one who was out all night, God knows where, doing God knows what. He went to his office party and came home. He was the husband who came home to be with the girls.

He would not forgive, would not forget.

The tension in the house lasted for weeks. It was intolerable for both of them, for all four of them, but he didn't know what to do to make it right. His wife had been out all night, and she wouldn't apologize; she wouldn't explain. That only made him believe the worst.

Their cracked marriage was about to dissolve.

Then one night Chrissie took matters into her own hands. He woke up to her quietly, slowly, sweetly, taking his penis into her mouth. She worked it so expertly—almost lovingly—that he had no choice but to forgive her for whatever it was they'd been fighting about.

Their sex life had not been all that great after several years of marriage and two children, but that night harkened back to their honeymoon days in beautiful Ireland. It was hot, juicy, sexy, tantalizing. They played give and take for hours, and when it was over for each of them, they slept entwined until the alarm clock went off.

From that morning on, they were a family again. All the events of New Year's Eve had been put behind them.

Eventually, Chrissie revealed that she was pregnant.

Adam was furious. They'd been so careful! How could this have happened?

Chrissie shrugged it off, blaming that wild hot night in January. But Adam was suspicious, and rightly so.

Monica Sue, a.k.a. Mouse, was born early with long, thick black hair, not like Adam, who had less hair than he had a year ago, and it was a soft brown. Mouse's hair was not at all like Chrissie's dishwater blonde hair, or the fair hair of her sisters. No, Monica Sue looked like nobody in either family that Adam could name.

Even his parents pointed that out to him, quietly, privately.

When he mentioned their comments to Chrissie, she laughed it off, telling him they were all silly. "All our daughters are different from one another," she said, more than once. "Look at our Mouse. So healthy. So adorable. Let's be grateful she wasn't born like the Wilson's daughter." Or the Sapkowski's daughter, or Todd and Amy's son, or any of the children Chrissie knew of who were born with difficulties.

Mouse was healthy and curious, and that curiosity got her into the mischief that became the hallmark of her personality.

But Adam knew. He knew Mouse had been conceived on New Year's Eve, and not in his bed. He had seen the name Oliver on Chrissie's phone, knew that he was her coworker, saw that she smiled now and then in a private way when she got a text message, and when questioned, she erased it and blew it off as if it was nothing.

Adam knew the meaning of that secret smile.

But he swallowed it for the good of the family, and gave Mouse to Chrissie—another daughter for her to raise—while he spent more time and still more time with Lisa, his favorite.

Now that he'd seen Oliver up close and personal, he knew it all for certain, because Mouse looked exactly like that snake in the dining room.

Surely Mouse and Sonja had been permanently scarred by his indifference to them. Indifference, surely, to Sonja, but at times he had been downright mean to Mouse. Her punishments were always harsher, his words to her never loving or tender. Perhaps even Lisa hated him for ignoring his sisters and so blatantly preferring her over them. How could he possibly put his family back together?

Maybe it would be best if he never woke up from this nightmare.

He had always thought of himself as a good man, a good father, a good husband, a good employee, but in fact he was none of those things. It took a nightmare in a tunnel for him to realize it.

Slowly, he brought his cold hands up to his hot face.

He rubbed his face, squinting his eyes closed and wishing for a do-over.

Magic!

Could he have a do-over? Could he petition Jolmy's underworld gods for a time machine?

He could go back to that New Year's Eve.

No, *further*.

He would go back to the day Sonja was born.

No, *earlier*.

He would go back to the first time Chrissie asked for another baby. He would embrace that notion and then embrace her and then embrace Sonja, and they would be a complete family. Mouse, when she came along two years later, would look like him, not like some swarthy, dark-haired jackass co-worker of Chrissie's.

He had three cards left in his pocket.

He was still rocketing feet first through dark black water in his little cocoon of breathable air, sliding around rocks, falling over waterfalls, and swirling in and out of eddies and currents. He had given up fighting it. He just relaxed, and let the current take him.

The blue light on his chest would soon begin to sputter and then die, and when it did, he would lose his bubble of protection against the blackness, against the water.

He would be smashed against the rocks. He would drown.

Nobody would ever know what happened to him.

The girls would think he had abandoned them. So would his company, and so would the Justice Corps. It would be seven years before the courts would declare him dead and Chrissie could claim his life insurance. If she could afford to keep up the payments on the policy.

By that time, she could be bankrupt. Destitute.

By that time, Lisa would be out of college, if she had the money to go to college without his paycheck. By that time, Sonja would be in college, if Chrissie had the funds. And Mouse would be a senior in high school.

But Chrissie would have no funds. Adam had squandered them. The casino had taken his weak ass and wrung it dry.

His employer paid his salary while he was doing this year in the Justice Corps, because it was a humanitarian effort that his company supported. But they would quickly stop that if he stopped coming to work.

What the fuck had he been thinking?

Slowly, carefully, so as not to disturb the bubble that seemed so fragile and yet was clearly tougher than any vinyl he knew, he unbuttoned the breast pocket in his shirt.

He couldn't control his life, he couldn't control this dream, he couldn't control his path down this furious river in his little magical submarine, he couldn't control his family's reaction to his stupidity … he couldn't control himself. For the first time ever, he let go of trying to control anything.

Three cards left. He pulled out one and held it up to the blue light.

It was hard to read without his glasses. He squinted.

Oh. The Hanged Man.

He barked a laugh. Hoist by his own petard. Hanging by his heels, at the mercy of the fates.

Wasn't that the goddamned truth?

Again, he had two choices. He could let the current carry him until the blue light winked out and he died—drowned or smashed on the rocks. Someday, on some beach, somebody would find his tiny corpse. Or his tiny bones. Or maybe when he died, the magic would disappear, he would grow back to normal size and his remains would get stuck in this aquifer and eventually rot to shreds.

Is that the sacrifice Jolmy's underworld gods wanted from him?

Or, he could throw a card while the blue light still burned, while the bubble still protected him and run the risk of the blast ripping the bubble apart.

This was a moment just exactly like the one he'd had before he jumped into the water from that cliff where the serpents left him. He wanted to sit and contemplate it. He wanted to review his life, to make amends in his heart, to beg forgiveness.

But the people from whom he needed to beg that forgiveness were not here. They could not hear him. They could not feel him.

He could not die in this underground river of water. He needed to make things as right as he possibly could, as long as there was breath left in him.

"Time machine," he whispered to the Hanged Man. "Or else just get me home. Please, God—any god—let me get out of here."

In a flash of understanding, he realized the magic had exacted its price: Self-revelation. He was a shitbird of the worst kind, always had been, and he knew it now like he had never known it before.

Was that the same as the underworld gods demanding their sacrifice? Was the sacrifice of his self-esteem enough for them?

Maybe, maybe not.

He tensed his muscles, ready for the bubble to disappear and plop him into the cold water. He took a deep breath, held it, then popped the card against the bubble wall in the tiny space allotted. The blue concentric rings fanned out, but he felt no concussion.

Immediately, though, the current smoothed out and he floated calmly, quietly, in what seemed to be a giant lake.

Still dark. Still black. Still underwater. He could only see his own dirty, raggedy self in the blue glow of his companion light.

He was completely helpless. He could not swim. He could not rise to the surface to see if there was breathable air there, and he could not dive to the bottom to kick off, or to see if he was in gravel or bedrock or what.

He could only float in place.

Would he soon run out of air?

The dark taste of claustrophobia hit the back of his tongue and he had a hard time catching his breath. There *wasn't* enough air!

He rolled over, and the bubble moved as he would expect it to move.

He tried to put a hand through it, to stretch it out enough that he could paddle, or move himself. Something, anything to direct his own fate.

Ha. That was a laugh.

He had done plenty to direct his own fate.

And now here he was, the size of a rat, stuck in a plastic bubble, floating helplessly in an aquifer.

The blue light began to sputter.

Great.

Adrenaline flushed through him.

This was it. This was the end. This was how he would die.

He reached into his pocket. Two cards left. Two cards, plus …

He pulled them out. Two cards: The Queen of Coins, and Judgment, along with the photo of his wife and daughters.

He didn't know what those artsy cards meant to his life, but he knew what the photo meant. He stuffed them back into his pocket.

Again, his bubble began to move. It picked up speed, as the blue light began to falter.

But this was different. This didn't feel like the same kind of current.

He lifted his head and saw a tiny glint of metal ahead, illuminated by the light he carried on his chest.

The blue flame flared.

Adam took a big gasp of air and held his breath.

The flame went out, the bubble popped, and he was again in water, cold water, being drawn rapidly toward the metal he had glimpsed.

Where there was metal, there would be civilization.

His speed picked up as the metal drew him to it.

Just as he thought he must be able to reach out and grasp it, the current stopped and reversed, blowing Adam backward in a torrent of bubbles. Adam tumbled in the black water, desperately trying to hold onto his lungful of air.

Bubbles!

Bubbles moved past him, past his face. He kicked his feet, swam hard and fast, following the bubbles up. He kicked again and his head broke through into a small breathing space of air.

He took great gulps of air, his heart thundering.

He grasped for a handhold, but there was nothing but sheer, smooth rock above him. His breath echoed loudly in the tiny air space. His nose touched the ceiling, his ears still underwater.

He breathed slowly, purposefully.

He needed to calm his heart. He needed to hold his breath again and investigate the metal pipe or whatever it was that was breathing water in and out.

He had two cards left. Two cards and the photo of his family, the inspiration that gave him the will to keep fighting.

Bubbles stopped popping around him, and the current shifted, pulling him back down.

He took a last deep breath and held it as he was sucked under, back toward the metal thing, and when he got to it, its force of suction plastered his chest, arms, legs to it with such force that he could barely move.

In a flash of insight, he knew exactly what it was, and then he knew where he was.

He was stuck to the filter screen on the well pump that he and Jolmy and the crew had installed.

He was directly below the village!

That explained the "respiration." They were testing the well. They pumped water up, and then they flushed it back down. They'd repeat that several times before they did the final assembly of the water system.

Lungs aching, stuck to the metal mesh by the force of the water it was drawing in, Adam moved his hand inch by desperate inch until he reached his pocket. He pulled out a card, but before he could deliberately do something with it, the rushing water sucked it out of his hand.

Still, the blue concussion sent out a great burp of water, and Adam slipped easily through the tiny holes in the screen.

Wait. *What?*

Not even particles of sand could go through that screen.

Oh. The magic had made him smaller yet. He had to be the size of a microbe.

The pump drew him up through the well shaft.

His lungs ached for a breath of air.

Panic built in his chest. His face reddened, his eyes bulged.

Hold on, hold on, hold on.

Surely sunlight was just ahead. Fresh air. Jolmy. Chrissie. The girls.

Hold on, hold on, hold on.

Then he realized that though he was only the size of bacteria, his next destination was not fresh air.

He was headed for the chlorination tank.

11

THERE WAS NOTHING for him to do now, except relax.

Relax and try to hold the lungful of air he had, until he could hold it no more.

Or until he was hit with a blast of chlorine that was designed to extinguish microbial life.

Just like him.

Or until they flushed the pipe again and he was swept back down into the aquifer, to be swept away and drown.

Regardless, there was nothing to fight. All he could do was close his eyes and try to dream himself home again.

His head popped up into a reservoir of air. He gulped it, gasped, drew it in.

Some kind of light source made everything fuzzy, out of focus, but he could see that there was light in the dimness.

At last.

Things started pulling on his legs, his arms. He bounced into and off of other soft body microorganisms, like rotifers, or bacteria. They stuck to him, sucked on him, tasting him, maybe attracted by the rotting flesh on his feet, looking for a meal. He would be no meal for them.

He punched them away, but every action had an equal and opposite reaction, as Lisa would tell him, and he had to find balance between keeping them away from him and keeping his head above water. He wanted to float in peace, but the little critters wouldn't leave him alone.

He worked his arms and legs hard to stay afloat while he kicked at them.

Then he pulled the final card from his pocket, but before he could formulate a wish or a prayer or whatever the hell it was that made the magic work in this place, again it was swept from his hand.

Far away, he thought he detected a minor jolt.

He just kept treading water.

He put his face up into the air bubble, took one final gasp of air, and held it in his lungs, waiting for something to happen.

Something always happened.

Sure enough, a moment later, the pipe he was in became smaller and smaller, and soon he could crawl through it on his hands and knees.

He was growing.

He didn't get far before he grew too big to fit in the pipe. He stretched his arms and legs out, wiggling forward, and still he grew.

He tried to envision the schematic of the water system they were installing. He had only designed part of it, so he had to work to remember it.

He could see it in his mind's eye, the blueprints laid out on a sheet of plywood resting on saw horses in the sun, corners held down from the hot summer winds by rocks and pieces of old brick and broken pottery.

He saw the PVC lines that led from the central spigot at the village all the way to the massive chemical treatment tanks situated close to the well head. Saw the pump in the middle of a big, fairly deep mud pit, saw the men in their hard hats with their dirty clothes and their wrenches, tracing pipes on the paper with work-hardened hands and dirty, cracked fingernails.

The pipe he was in got smaller and smaller.

If they were still testing the well, then they had not yet hooked it up to the chemical treatment tank.

He had to be in a pipe between the well and … and what, the pump?

Or maybe he was inside the pump.

If he was inside the pump when they started it up again, he'd be sliced to bits by the impeller. Not so bad if he was the size of a grain of sand, but he was big enough now to be killed by the twirling blades.

Stuck. Helpless.

Again, helpless.

He stopped growing. The pipe wasn't getting any smaller.

He had returned to the size of a rodent, and no water was getting past him in either direction. Water had drained down, leaving him gasping in breathable air.

The air smelled like the village. It tasted earthy, alive. It tasted like Africa.

It tasted like home.

Fortunately, that meant that he could take a couple of deep breaths, as the well was not yet a closed system.

Stuck, as if in a straight jacket, he wiggled his hand up until he could reach into his pocket.

The last card in his pocket was not a magic card at all, but the photo of Chrissie and the girls.

Those testing the well would know there was a clog somewhere and they would do something drastic about it any moment now.

However mystified, he knew they wouldn't cut the pipe. They wouldn't rip open the system. They would just flush it, to see if they could push the blockage out, one way or another.

Frantic, he wiggled around until he could pull the photo out of his pocket.

The Swan sisters and their mom. His Goddess Card.

"Please God," he said. "Please. God of Minnesota, God of Jolmy, God of the underworld, God of all religions everywhere. Give me a chance to make things right."

With the photo held between two fingers, he brought it up to his face, kissed it and flicked it against the pipe wall.

The blue concentric circles rocked him. Popped his ears.

He began to grow again.

He grew until he filled the pipe and then he continued to grow, though there was no space for him.

The air squeezed out of his lungs. Blood pressed into his head. He feared his skull would explode from the pressure.

Then the PVC pipe cracked, and he got a tiny bit of relief.

He flexed his muscles, pushed out with his arms, but he was so weak he made little headway.

The crack in the pipe ran a little longer, the space opened a bit wider.

Was he finally going to return to his normal size?

Mud flooded into the crack in the pipe, and he knew exactly where he was.

He was in the mud pit that surrounded the well.

He grabbed a last deep breath of air, before mud filled the pipe.

He fought to remain conscious as his growing head painfully spread the crack in the pipe open even wider. The darkness of unconsciousness began to swirl in the periphery of his vision. Red orbs floated in front of his eyes.

He fought it off, but he was running out of air.

The pipe cracked open wide enough for him to get a hand through.

The mud pit wasn't that deep, but mud washed in over his face, into his nose and mouth.

It tasted like blood.

He struggled to get an arm through the crack in the pipe. As the crack widened, he got an arm out and stuck out his hand.

Air! Dry air!

He waved his arm, wiggled his fingers, but as they slowly grew from the size of a rodent's paw, his oxygen-starved body began to fail. A darkness, darker than even the tunnels he had endured, closed in, obscuring even the red globules that had floated in front of his closed eyes.

His muscles weakened, began to fail.

He was out of air. His lungs couldn't hold out any longer. In a moment he would breathe in a big, gasping lungful of mud.

Or was it blood?

Occam's razor.

The simplest explanation was likely the right explanation.

Adam's miserable, fucked up life had just flashed before him.

Another fierce, booted kick to his chest slammed him back to reality.

He opened his eyes and found himself helpless on the dirt road next to the Jeep's tire. With grave understanding, he watched, powerless, as the thug's baton came down on his head a second time.

About the Author

Elizabeth Engstrom is a sought-after teacher and keynote speaker at writing conferences, conventions, and seminars around the world. She has written fifteen books and edited or co-edited eight anthologies. She has over two hundred fifty short stories, articles and essays in print. Her most recent nonfiction book is *How to Write a Sizzling Sex Scene*. Her book *Candyland* was recently made into a major motion picture, "Candiland", starring Gary Busey, Chelah Horsdal, and James Clayton. Engstrom lives in the Pacific Northwest with her fisherman-husband and their dog, where she teaches the occasional writing class, puts her pen to use for social justice, and is always working on her next book.

elizabethengstrom.com

The Original

DUNGEON SOLITAIRE

Tomb of Four Kings

Still Available for Free

at

matthewlowes.com/games

Complete Rules
are Print-Ready and Playable
with any Standard Deck
of Playing Cards

Dungeon Solitaire
Labyrinth of Souls

TAROT CARD GAME

by MATTHEW LOWES

Illustrated by JOSEPHE VANDEL

Complete Rulebook
&
Labyrinth of Souls Tarot Deck
Available at
matthewlowes.com/games

Labyrinth of Souls Fiction
Coming Soon

Symphony of Ruin by Christina Lay
The End of All Things by Matthew Lowes
Bayou's Lament by Cheryl Owen-Wilson
Exhumation of the Divine by Pamela Jean Herber

... and more to come!

information at

shadowspinnerspress.com